To Spence
with best wishes..

Philip Caveney
2014

1

BREAKFAST IN BEIRUT

PHILIP CAINE

BREAKFAST IN BEIRUT

First paperback edition printed 2016 in the United Kingdom

ISBN 9780993374821

Published by PHILIP CAINE
philcaine777@hotmail.com

For more copies of this book, please email:
philcaine777@hotmail.com

Editor: Gillian Ogilvie

Cover Design: www.gonzodesign.co.uk

Printed in Great Britain by:
Orbital Print www.orbitalprint.co.uk

4

ABOUT THE AUTHOR

Philip has over thirty five years' experience, operating projects across 3 continents, within the Oil & Gas Industry, providing support in facilitates & project management, to blue chip clients, in remote and hazardous locations.

His career began in hotel management and then transitioned to offshore North Sea, where he worked the boom years on Oil Rigs, Barges & Platforms. Fifteen years passed and Philip returned to onshore projects taking a three year contract to manage accommodation bases in North & West Africa.

From Africa Philip moved to the 'Former Soviet Union' where he managed & directed multiple projects in Kazakhstan & Russia, again supporting the Oil industry; a particularly exciting seven years where dealings with the KGB were an everyday event.

The end of the Iraq War in 2003 produced a change of client that took Philip to Baghdad, where, as Operations Director, he controlled the operations & project management, of multiple accommodation bases for the American Military. A challenging, hazardous & demanding location that required him to provide and deliver full support for over 30,000 troops, on nine separate locations, throughout Baghdad and Northern Iraq. Signing up for an initial six months he ended up staying seven years.

The last three years of his career were spent running a couple of support services companies in Iraq with head offices in Dubai, a rare treat indeed for Philip to be able to have his family with him in such a wonderful city.

Philip semi-retired in 2014 and began writing in February 2015, after joining Ulverston Writers Group. His first novel, PICNIC IN IRAQ tells a story of a group of close friends who travel the length of Iraq in search of a treasure of unimaginable wealth. The sequel TO CATCH A FOX is an exciting rescue mission set in Syria. BREAKFAST IN BEIRUT is his third novel.

http://philcaine777.wix.com/philipcaine

Also by Philip Caine

PICNIC IN IRAQ

TO CATCH A FOX

The only thing necessary for the triumph of evil
is for good men to do nothing.

Edmund Burke....

BREAKFAST IN BEIRUT
Prologue
March 2009

Tahir Suri had worked as an engineer at the Chasma
Nuclear Power Station since it went online in 2000. The
plant, the first of five in Punjab province, provided
electricity for over half a million homes in the northern
region of Pakistan.

Tahir, a husband and father of six young sons was
dying of bowel cancer. His life with his family had been
a modest one and his salary, though much bigger than
most in Pakistan, did not enable him to save for the
future of his loved ones. His condition was terminal and
he knew he would not see out the summer.

The stranger had offered him a way to provide for his
family, a way for them to be kept in comfort and security
for the rest of their lives. The money promised was more
than enough for a new home, enough to send all his sons
to university, perhaps even to send them to Europe.

It had not been easy for him to remove the material
and he knew he was taking the greatest risk, but why not,
the risk was worth the reward for his beloved family. He
was lead- shift engineer in the plant and he was able to
conceal the material in a small lead lined case, which
fitted snugly into his rucksack. Even in the cool of the

evening, he sweated profusely as he walked through the last security gate and out to the car park. He found his old Nissan and placed the bag in the boot, then drove slowly out of the workers' parking area and onto the main road north.

The drive to meet the stranger would take a little over an hour. He was tired after the long shift and the pain in his stomach was making him nauseous, but he did not stop. It was dark when he arrived at the mouth of the Pashtun Valley. He pulled over next to the old travellers' shelter, got out of the car and stretched the muscles in his back. Taking a battered thermos flask from the glove box, he poured some of the contents into the cup. From a small plastic container he removed two capsules and washed the medication down with cold tea. As he replaced the thermos he was startled for a second by the headlights of an approaching vehicle.

'Salam Alaikum, Tahir,' said the stranger.

'Alaikum Salam,' he replied, as he went to the boot of the old Nissan.

'You have done well my friend,' said the stranger, 'and you have secured the future of your family.

'Inshallah,' said Tahir, as he handed the rucksack to the man, 'You have the other half of my money, sir?'

'Yes yes, I have your money my friend. It's in my car.'

The stranger carefully concealed the bag in the boot of his vehicle and then turned back to Tahir. A single gunshot echoed up the Pashtun Valley, as the bullet entered the engineer's forehead.

Chapter One
May 13th 2009
'Casino Rafael'

Farida Mancini was born in Cairo to a Lebanese mother and Sicilian father. At thirty-four she was tall with a figure women envied and men desired. Her long black hair framed the tanned face; the huge dark eyes and full lips made her truly beautiful. It was a few minutes after midnight and the Casino Rafael, overlooking the Beirut Marina, was busy with high roller gamblers and wealthy VIP's. At the bar, Farida sipped her champagne and waited impatiently.

Jack Castle pulled up to the front of the casino in the hired Aston Martin. Before leaving the vehicle he clipped the single handcuff to his left wrist. The other end of the security chain was attached to a slim reinforced aluminium briefcase. He left the engine running as he stepped out of the vehicle and waited a few seconds until the parking valet arrived. The young Asian smiled and handed him a small slip of paper, 'Good evening, sir. Welcome to the Rafael.'
   'Thank you,' said Jack. 'Please keep it close by, I won't be here very long. The name is Sterling.'
   Jack hadn't been to Lebanon for many years, not since before the troubles back in the eighties and nineties, but he was impressed with how the city had regenerated itself, even in today's difficult times. He

12

walked through the opulent foyer and into the main casino area, then stood and looked around the elegant room. The huge floor to ceiling windows at the rear of the casino overlooked the marina and in front of the windows the bar stretched the whole width of the gambling area. He had never met Farida Mancini before, but the description he'd been given did not match the woman he was looking at, beautiful, elegant, mysterious.

'Good evening, Miss Mancini.'

She looked at the Cartier watch on her slim wrist, 'Good morning, Mr Sterling.'

With a smile and nod of his head, he replied, 'Ah, yes of course, sorry I'm late. Please call me Jack.'

'Very well, Jack. I'm Farida. Can I get you a drink?'

'Nothing for me at the moment, thank you,' then with a smile he continued, 'perhaps after we've discussed our business. I assume that will not be here of course.'

She picked up the crystal flute and took another sip of champagne. After putting the glass back on the bar she looked him up and down, then nodded towards the window, 'The biggest yacht, moored against the end of the jetty.'

Jack turned and looked out of the windows across the floodlit marina and the millions of dollars' worth of sleek seagoing vessels. He turned back to the woman, 'Beautiful lines.'

She smiled at his double meaning, finished her champagne, then gracefully stepped off the barstool. 'Mr Shahadi is on-board. Before we go may I please see your entrance fee?'

He smiled at the terminology and placed the case on the bar. He looked around to ensure no one was paying any attention, then spun the lock tumblers and clicked open the lid.

The woman reached into the case and discreetly flipped through the bundle of certificates. 'All there, Mr Sterling,' she said with a slight smile, 'Jack.'

As he closed the case he said quietly, 'Yes indeed, ten million dollars in bearer bonds.'

In his early fifties, Jack Castle was tall, reasonably fit and healthy. Greying hair complemented sparkling brown eyes that gave a light to his tanned face. He had a good sense of humour and an infectious personality most people liked. His happy childhood had been spent in England's Lake District and he was the elder of two brothers. His father and mother had been doctors in the little town of Windermere and it was his father who had taught Jack the meaning and value of responsibility, loyalty and honour. He learned the importance of love, kindness, and respect, from his mother.

When he was twenty Jack's parents had tragically died in a car accident and it was this which caused Jack to abandon the idea of becoming a doctor, electing to join the British Army instead. He'd spent fifteen years in the military trying to overcome the guilt and anger he harboured following the death of his parents. He worked hard and rose to the rank of captain in the Special Air Service, after which his friend, Tom Hillman, had convinced him private security was the way forward and in 1993 Jack began working with Tom as personal protection officers, for high paying clients.

Ten years on and it was Jack who owned the security company, with several key contracts in various conflict zones across the world. In 2003 they had set up in Baghdad and had secured a dozen major clients in Iraq, Kurdistan and the Emirates.

After the success of the recent Syrian job and with his experience and contacts in that part of the world, not to mention Russia, Jack had been approached by British Intelligence. His brother Mathew was now Head of Operations for the Middle East and it was he who had persuaded Jack to work for MI6 on an ad-hoc basis. Jack's first mission was Lebanon.

Chapter Two
2 Days Earlier
'Arrivals'

Beirut's Rafic Hariri Airport is Lebanon's only international airport and the home of Middle East Airlines. Flight MEA-19 had left Heathrow almost an hour late, but the trip had been comfortable enough and although Jack had experienced better service on other business class flights, the staff had been attentive and the food edible. As the aircraft made its approach to Beirut it reduced altitude and levelled off at three hundred feet above the sparkling Mediterranean. The big wheels bumped onto the tarmac and, as the pilot reversed thrust, the plane slowed in a somewhat unnecessary fashion causing a couple of the older passengers to utter a few short words of prayer. Pulling up to the walkway, flight MEA-19 came to a halt with a sudden jerk, resulting in several already standing passengers to be knocked off their feet. *Muppets,* thought Jack, as he returned the smile from the stewardess.

Tom was already at the airport, having flown in from Dubai earlier in the day. In the bar he watched the Arrivals Board as it changed and declared the London flight had arrived. He finished his beer, left the crowded bar and made his way to the Arrivals area.

Tom Hillman was Jack Castle's closest friend and business partner; they had met over twenty years ago in the Balkans. Tom had been with Military Intelligence at that time and was attached to Jack's SAS team to neutralise an Armenian warlord who'd been operating independently on the Armenian, Kosovo border. The mission had resulted in the warlord being killed by a single long-distance shot from Tom, a result both men thought highly appropriate, given the Armenian's history for killing refugees. They had been friends and colleagues ever since.

Tom was a few years younger than Jack, slightly shorter and slimmer, with close cropped fair hair, tanned face and blue eyes. Born in the UK, he'd spent most of his younger life in Leeds. He had two daughters from a previous marriage, but his home now was Dubai, where he lived on 'The Palm' with his second wife Helen. Although he and Jack still ran their company, Tom always spent as much time as he could, out in the Gulf on his sixty foot yacht.

Jack had moved quickly through the disembarking crowd and by the time he'd reached Immigration he was first through the desk. He'd only travelled with a small carry-on wheelie, so the Customs process was equally swift. As he left the air-conditioned Customs area and entered the public Arrivals Hall the heat hit him. He stood for a few seconds and then saw Tom waving. Jack made his way through the throng of friends and families waiting for their loved ones and pushed his way to the exit. Tom had moved outside to get away from the crowd as Jack exited the building.

'How're you doing, mate?' said Tom with a grin.

Jack smiled and they shook hands, 'Good to see you, buddy.'

With a wave of his hand Tom said, 'Car's this way. Let's get the hell outta here.'

As they arrived at the parking area Tom clicked the remote and the lights on a new Aston Martin Vantage flashed.

Jack smiled, 'Oh, nice one, Tom.'

'Well you did say we'd need something classy.'

Not wishing to stay in one of the big five star hostelries in the city, Jack had asked his friend to look for something less obvious. About five kilometres north of Beirut and overlooking the Mediterranean, the recently opened Phoenix Boutique Hotel fitted the bill perfectly; small, classy and discreet.

The drive from the airport took them along the esplanade and north out of the city and although the roads were busy they arrived at the hotel a little after five in the afternoon. As they pulled up under the small portico a liveried valet appeared along with a second attendant pushing a small luggage trolley.

'Good afternoon, gentlemen. Welcome to The Phoenix. We hope you will have a pleasant stay.'

After taking their bags from the boot and placing them on the trolley, the valet drove off in the Aston while the porter accompanied them to the reception desk. Once checked in, and as they rode the lift to the third floor, Jack said, 'What time's your meeting with your old pal?'

Tom waited a few seconds as the lift arrived at their floor and as they stepped out said, 'Ten o-clock in the old port. I'll brief you when we get settled in.'

The porter opened Jack's door first, stood back to let him in and then offloaded his bags onto the stand. Jack handed him a five pound note and the porter beamed a 'Thank you, sir.'

Tom said, 'See you in a few minutes,' as he and the porter moved on to the next room.

Jack went onto the balcony took out his smartphone and checked for a signal, then hit the speed dial for his wife Nicole. After two rings he heard her voice and the pet name she always called him when he was away from her, 'Zaikin, you've arrived safely?'

'Hi, darling. Yes, arrived okay. I'm here at the hotel with Tom.'

Nicole Elizabeth Orlova was born of an English mother and Russian father. She and Jack had been together for over sixteen years, the last of which as man and wife. At thirty six she had inherited her dead mother's beauty and her father's shrewd brain. In her younger years she had been a very successful fashion model, but now was a respected business woman with a chain of spas and a very lucrative property portfolio in England. Her father was the billionaire Russian oligarch, Dimitri Mikhailovich Orlov.

'When do you think you'll be home?'

'Not sure yet, but not more than a week I hope.'

'Me too,'

A knock on the door brought the conversation to an end, 'Tom's here. I gotta go, darling.'

'Okay, Zaikin, be careful. I love you.'

'Love you too, baby. Talk soon.'

Jack opened the door, 'Sorry, was just talking to Nikki.'

'How is she?

'She's fine, buddy. You want a drink?'

'Yeah. Is there beer?'

Jack opened the mini bar and took out a cola and a beer. 'So, Tom. Tell me all about your old pal in Hamas!'

Chapter Three
'The Old Turk'

The old port of Beirut is more of a tourist attraction now, as opposed to the working port it once was and the main docks area to the south end of the bay has gone through a massive industrialisation. Where once old warehouses and quays used to bustle with small trucks, lorries and workers, container yards and purpose built loading docks now stand with automated cranes and gantries. The old port though; still retains its cosmopolitan quirkiness and has many restaurants, cafes and bars, where the braver tourists may venture and the local populous gather to relieve them of their hard earned holiday spending money.

'The Old Turk' café bar is set back from the main promenade, at the end of a narrow secluded side street. This is one establishment that very rarely entices a tourist to enter. With its dark booths and thick smoky atmosphere it reeked of a time gone by, when Lascars, pirates and sailors of every nationality would be the usual clientele. In an attempt to entice the more adventurous of modern tourist, a twice nightly show was offered with the star attraction being a rather voluptuous pair of ladies performing the local style of belly dance.

It was a few minutes before ten when Tom entered the café. Disregarding the offer of a drink from the heavy-set barman and the services of an equally heavy-set prostitute, he made his way to the back of the dimly lit room.

Akim al Hashem, known only to his closest friends as 'Aki' was seated in the last booth, stirring a glass of steaming tea. He nodded as Tom approached, but did not stand or shake hands, nor did he draw any attention to their meeting. Tom sat down as a young waiter arrived. 'Bottled water, please. And leave the top on.'

'Salaam Alaikum, my old friend. How have you been?'

'Salaam,' replied Tom, 'I'm well, Aki. And you, your family, all well?'

Hashem was in his mid-forties and with his broad shoulders and stocky frame he could have passed for a wrestler. His pleasant tanned face was marred by a thick white scar that ran from the side of his left eye down his cheek to the jawline.

In 1995, Tom had been on secondment in Palestine with the local security services. They had been watching a small block of apartments that was allegedly an insurgent stronghold. Tom had picked up the original information but, after passing it on to the local security, the chain of command had been compromised and the intelligence was distorted. Nevertheless the team had gone into the building and routed several families resulting in the deaths of several innocent individuals. Realising the operation was flawed Tom had tried to stop the local security from continuing the assault on the building, but without success. Tom had entered one of the apartments and found Akim al Hashem hiding in a back room, with his pregnant wife and young son. Not wishing to see more innocents killed he'd helped the family escape the area and out of harm's way. Before vanishing into the night, Akim swore he would always be beholden to Tom for the kindness he had shown and for saving the lives of his family. Over the years he and Tom had stayed in touch and even when Hashem had joined Hamas, they'd continued to be friends.

The waiter returned with the water and after cracking the seal Tom wiped the top of the bottle and swallowed half the contents, then looked across the table. Akim met his gaze with a serious expression. 'It's good to see you, Tom, but I'm sure this is not a social visit. What can I do for you my, friend?'

Tom smiled and looked around the room. No one was paying them any interest as the gyrations of the first belly dancer held their undivided attention.

'So, Aki, what can you tell me about stolen Pakistani plutonium, my friend?'

Chapter Four
'Golden Cloud'

Jack handed the slip of paper to the valet and watched as the young Asian rushed off to retrieve his car. As the Aston Martin pulled up in front of them, Farida smiled and said, 'Beautiful car.'

As he held the door open, she slipped elegantly into the low seat and smiled again as she caught him admiring her long legs. Jack hand the valet a large tip, which resulted in a delighted, 'Thank you sir,' from the beaming attendant.

The powerful engine growled as they left the driveway and drove out onto the promenade road. Jack checked the rear view mirror and saw the black Range Rover following about twenty yards behind them. A few minutes later the Aston was waved through the entrance to the dock area by a uniformed security guard. Jack checked the rear mirror again and saw the black Range Rover slow down, then speed up and drive away to the north.

Shahadi's yacht was the largest and clearly the most expensive in the marina. 'Golden Cloud' was an international seagoing vessel, a one hundred and sixty feet long man-made thing of beauty. The gleaming white hull and superstructure were illuminated by spotlights on the dock and shone like a beacon in the dark Lebanese night. On the rear deck stood a pair of matching helicopters promoting Jack's comment, 'Oh, how cute. His-n-hers choppers.'

As they approached Golden Cloud, they passed another smaller yacht with about two dozen people partying the night away. Jack smiled at the name emblazoned on the stern of the ship; 'Dragon's Breath.' Above the name was an ornate depiction of a dragon's head spitting flame from its mouth.

As they pulled up to the end of the jetty the car was stopped by one of Shahadi's own security personnel. Recognising Farida in the passenger seat the guard quickly moved to her door and opened it with a flourish. As he offered his hand for her to exit he said, 'Good evening, Miss Mancini.'

She left the car and walked to a small portable reception desk at the foot of the gangway.

Jack parked the car next to several other high end vehicles and nodded to the clutch of chauffeur-bodyguards who seemed more intent on watching Farida than acknowledging him. At the desk stood two more of Shahadi's armed guards.

'You'll need to be searched, Jack,' she said almost apologetically.

'Yes, of course.'

He held his arms out as one of the guards ran a metal detector expertly and efficiently over Jack's arms, torso and legs. Lifting the back of his jacket the guard removed a small automatic from Jack's waistband. 'We'll hold onto this, sir. Please open the case.'

Jack placed the case on the small desk and quickly spun the tumblers. The guard checked the contents and when satisfied there was no threat said, 'Thank you, sir. Welcome to the Golden Cloud.'

As they walked aboard he saw two more armed guards at the top of the gangway and noticed two more at the bow. *Probably guards on the starboard side and at the stern*, he thought to himself. *Shahadi isn't taking any chances But then again he is the biggest arms dealer in this part of the world.*

They walked along the highly polished deck to the rear of the vessel and Farida led the way into the opulent central salon. Half a dozen men were standing around talking and drinking and as the two entered a tall slim man split from the group and approached them. He wore a pale grey Armani linen suit over a light blue shirt. His dark hair had greyed at the sides and the hairline had receded considerably. He wore rimless spectacles balanced on the end of a hawkish nose. Smiling the man moved straight to Farida, kissed her cheek and said in a slightly annoyed tone, 'Darling, I wondered where you had got to. We're all waiting.'

'I'm sorry, sir,' said Jack, 'that's my fault. I was late. Please excuse my tardiness.'

'Ah, Mr Sterling. I am Vini Shahadi. Welcome to our little gathering. I believe you represent our friends in Ireland?'

Jack held out his right hand, 'Yes, indeed. Please call me, Jack.'

Shahadi disregarded the offered hand and request for informality and said, 'Yes, quite. Please join us. We will not be conducting introductions tonight. I think you'll appreciate the requirement for everyone's anonymity. I'm the only one that needs to know who is present.'

As Shahadi turned and re-joined the main group, Jack looked at Farida, raised an eyebrow and said, 'No warm welcomes then?'

She smiled, 'Just business I'm afraid.' She pointed towards a large dining table, 'Please leave your case with the others.'

Jack turned and moved to the big table, unlocked the handcuff and as he placed his case next to five other similar pieces of luggage thought, *sixty million dollars, just sitting there!*

Shahadi had resumed his position at the front of the elegant salon, 'Gentlemen, tonight we welcome you all, one representative from each of the interested parties. It is not necessary for you to know who is who, but I can tell you that you will be bidding live against each other. Represented are Hamas, Hezbollah, Al Qaeda, the PLO, and our new friends from ISIL. We also have a representative of our old friends in Ireland. You are all aware of the immense value of what you are about to bid on. Due to the extremely hazardous nature of the material, I'm sure you will appreciate the risk in a hands-on viewing.' Shahadi smiled as the group of buyers nodded. 'Therefore I have arranged for my technicians to verify the product for you. You all know my reputation for the quality of the goods I supply. So you may be confident when I tell you this material is of the highest standard with its origin being the Chasma Power Station in Pakistan.'

Several of the group nodded and smiled at the arms dealers reference to the recent theft from the power plant. Farida had joined Shahadi and said, 'Gentlemen, if

I can have your attention please,' the wall behind her slid open to reveal a ninety inch television screen. She used a remote control and switched on the set. The picture showed a laboratory scene with two technicians in full radiation protection. One technician had his hands in large rubber gloves that were attached to a protective Perspex case. Inside the case was a smaller yellow container with several nuclear warning signs emblazoned on the cover and sides. The gloved technician carefully opened the lid, as the second technician moved in with a small video camera. The open yellow container revealed what looked like a cylindrical block of grey material, six inches long and two inches in diameter. The cameraman zoomed in on the numbers stamped into the cylinder.

'Please note the numbers, gentlemen,' said Farida, 'you will see they match the data sheet we have provided for you.'

As the cameraman panned out, the gloved technician closed the container and the screen went blank.

Six laptops had been placed on separate tables around the room.

'Now, gentlemen,' continued Farida, 'if you would please take your seats in front of your designated computer. Each one of these has been linked to the screen in front of you. As you make your bids the amounts will be displayed on the screen. Your organisations will not be displayed, although we will of course know who is making the highest bid. You will only see who is top of the list and that is the price you will need to exceed to win the auction.'

One of the men asked, 'What about the ten million dollars we've already deposited?'

'Shahadi smiled a thin joyless smile, 'The successful bidder will have their ten million considered as deposit against their winning bid, the balance to be paid within three days. The rest will have their funds returned before you leave tonight.'

Another of the group asked, 'And if we can't make the balance of payment within three days? If we need more time?'

Again Shahadi smiled, 'Then you will lose your deposit and the next highest bidder will be contacted and given the option to buy the product.'

'Gentlemen, would anyone care for something else to drink before we begin?' said Farida.

'Let's get to it,' said one of the men impatiently.

'Very well, gentlemen.' said Shahadi, 'the opening bid will start at three hundred million dollars.'

Chapter Five
'Party People'

At the mouth of the harbour a sleek sixty foot motor launch eased slowly into the marina and then slowed almost to a stop, as the pilot, on slow engines, held the vessel expertly in position. The 'Magma' rocked gently on the black waters, about one hundred yards from Golden Cloud. The woman in the wheel house raised a small set of binoculars to her eyes and scanned the length of the gleaming white ship moored against the quayside and then turned the binoculars on the adjacent smaller vessel. She smiled as she watched the party people enjoying their evening. 'Hold her steady, Bennie. Won't be long now.'

* * *

The raucous party on Dragon's Breath had spilled out onto the quayside. A dozen or so men and women were dancing and singing up and down the jetty, drinking from bottles of champagne and generally making complete idiots of themselves; much to the amusement of the three armed guards at the foot of Golden Cloud's gangway. The group danced and sang and shouted to the guards to join them. The disturbance on the quayside quickly brought the rest of Shahadi's security men to the jetty-side of the ship and then realising it was only a group of drunks, watched from the deck as the revellers danced towards Golden Cloud's gangway.

The guards on the quayside took a defensive posture as the drunks approached, but were taken aback by the nearest woman, as she pulled down her low cut dress exposing her ample bosom. The guards on board laughed and shouted crude words of encouragement to their colleagues on the jetty. The rest of the Dragon's Breath party had now disembarked and were joining their friends alongside Golden Cloud. Seeing the crowd had grown and seemed to be getting out of hand, two of the on-board guards began walking down the gangway to assist.

Behind the woman with exposed breasts a man fired a silenced weapon, killing the nearest of the three men. At the first thump of the quiet gunshot the rest of the revellers all drew weapons and opened up on Shahadi's unsuspecting guards. With the three quayside men dead the attackers ran for the gangway firing silenced Uzi machine guns. The two men on the gangway fell over the side like synchronised divers, dead before they hit the water. The remaining six on-board guards returned fire with their AK47s. The earlier party atmosphere had now turned into a full blown gun battle.

At the first sound of the AK's Shahadi quickly took the remote control from Farida and closed off the main glass doors into the central salon.

'What the hell's going on?' screamed one of the group.

'We are obviously under attack, you idiot,' snapped another.

'Don't be alarmed, gentlemen,' said Shahadi calmly, 'the doors and the windows are all bullet proof. You will be quite safe in here.'

On the quayside and realising their bosses were under attack, the small group of chauffer-bodyguards attempted to join the firefight, but were quickly cut down by two Uzi-wielding women. The band of attackers surged forward, their superior numbers negating their exposed position, but nevertheless they still sustained several casualties. More than a dozen party goers were now on board the beleaguered ship, with several more running up the gangway. Shahadi's outnumbered guards fought to the last man and then silence returned, as the party people took over control of the ship.

* * *

The woman on board Magma, had watched as the attackers took over Golden Cloud, 'Okay, Bennie. Move in.'

The captain pushed the engine controls to sixty percent and the sleek vessel surged forward under the sudden burst of power. Within two minutes the smaller vessel was tied up alongside the captured arms dealer's yacht.

* * *

On the hilltop at the northern tip of the harbour, the black Range Rover was parked, its engine running and the air-conditioning on low. Tom Hillman had watched the events at the end of the jetty through powerful field glasses. The party people's assault on Golden Cloud and the smaller vessel arriving alongside were all unexpected events. He'd watched the gunfight and afterwards, as people moved from Shahadi's boat to the smaller ship alongside.

A few minutes later Tom saw one of Golden Cloud's helicopters fire up its engine, lift off and climb into the starlit sky. The chopper turned away from the marina and flew towards Tom's position on the hill top; he watched as the small aircraft flew overhead and away to the north.

The smaller vessel had eased away from Shahadi's yacht and sailed swiftly toward the mouth of the harbour. Tom could faintly hear the throb of the powerful engines carried on the sea breeze, as the sleek craft quickly vanished into the dark Mediterranean night. The faint sound of engines was soon replaced by the wailing of multiple police sirens approaching the marina. Tom put down the binoculars and stepped out of the cool vehicle into the warm air. He took out his smartphone and touched a speed-dial number, two rings later Mathew Sterling said, 'Good evening, Tom?'

'It's all gone tits up here, Matt.'

The wailing sirens grew louder and then were drowned out completely by the sound of the huge explosion that destroyed Golden Cloud.

Chapter Six
'Hello, Jack'

Jack felt the surge of the powerful engines as the ship's speed increased. The cable-ties binding his wrists cut into his flesh and the hood over his head was making him sweat, but he sat and waited for whatever was to come next. He was aware of another person in the room and said, 'What the fuck's going on?'

There was no reply from the other occupant, but a few minutes later he heard the door open and a woman's voice say, 'Okay, you can go. Thank you.'

The voice wasn't Farida's. It was American; the east coast accent seemed familiar.

'What the fucks going on?' he said again through the uncomfortable hood.

A warm hand held his wrist and he felt the cool of steel as a blade cut the cable-ties. The hood was removed and as his eyes adjusted to the bright lights of the small cabin, he saw Lisa Reynard standing in front of him.

'Hello, Jack. Good to see you again, honey.'

Born in new York and now in her late-thirties, Lisa Reynard was tall and athletic. Her olive skin and dark eyes a testament to her Italian heritage. She wore denim jeans and a loose fitting khaki shirt over a khaki T-shirt, her boots were US military issue. Her long hair was secured by the rear clasp of a New York Yankees baseball cap.

He remembered his first meeting with Lisa in Baghdad, 2003, when she was reporting for the Washington Post. They'd become friends and she had spoken of her varied career in many of the worlds conflict zones, mostly in Central Africa.

He said nothing for several seconds and then, 'Lisa! What the hell are you doing here?'

'I could ask you the same question, Mr Castle.'

He stood up and rubbed his wrists, moved over to the small side table and picked up a bottle of water, cracked the seal and drank half the contents, then looked at her, 'You know why I'm here, but I've just realized why you are. You're working for the Central Intelligence Agency.'

'Oh, Jack, I've missed you. You are so British. It's wonderful.'

'Are you taking the piss?'

'Never in a million years, honey. That was meant as a compliment.' As she moved towards him she opened her arms and said, 'You gonna gimme a hug then?'

A knock on the door broke their embrace. Lisa shouted, 'Come in,' and Farida Mancini entered the room. Her high heeled Christian Le Bouton's and the Versace dress had been replaced with trainers, jeans and a T-shirt, the long black her hair tied back in a ponytail.

'You okay, Jack? Sorry we were a little rough with you, but we needed to make it look convincing.'

'So you're bloody CIA as well?'

'Lisa will fill you in, Jack. But right now we need this cabin for some of the wounded.'

'Let's go up on deck,' said Lisa. 'See you later, Farida?'

'Sure, see you both later.'

* * *

Tom drove quickly back to their hotel. As soon as he entered his room he called Akim al Hashem. After several rings a sleepy voice said, 'Salaam, hello?'

'Aki, its Tom. I need to see you as soon as possible.'

'What time is it?'

'It's almost two o-clock.'

'I can meet you for breakfast in Beirut, Tom, but not now, my friend.'

'Okay that's fine. We're staying at . . .'

'I know where you are, Tom. I'll see you at nine.'

'Thanks, Aki.'

* * *

Out on deck, several of the party people sat around in small groups talking quietly, some checking weapons others were stretched out trying to sleep as the boat bounced over the dark waters of the Mediterranean. Jack looked at the moon and then the lights of the shore line a few miles away to the west, 'We're heading south.'

'That's right. We'll be in Haifa in about three hours.'

They moved to the bow, away from the noise of the powerful engines at the stern and sat down on the deck, their backs against the superstructure. Every now and then they were hit with a little spray as the sleek craft sped its way down the Lebanese coastline.

'So how long have you been with the CIA, Lisa?'

'Not CIA, Jack. NSA.'

'Same difference,' said Jack, somewhat indignantly, 'so how long have you worked for the National Security Agency?'

'It started several years ago. I did a couple of very minor jobs for the CIA when I was in Africa. Nothing extraordinary. A little intelligence gathering. Some surveillance work, that kinda thing. But after the two towers came down on nine-eleven, I was approached by the NSA to take a more active role. I was trained in basic field-craft and counter terrorist techniques. I did a lot of political science at college and my job as an international journalist provided viable cover. They considered me an asset and it went on from there.'

'Right, so what about last year when you joined us on the Iraq diamond job? Were you on mission then?'

'Oh no, honey. That was all me, your friend, and eager journalist.'

More spray hit them and, as they wiped their faces Jack said, 'And what about Miss Mancini? Is she CIA or NSA, or what?'

'Neither one. She's Mossad.'

'Oh, for fuck sake. Is anyone around here not a spook?'

'Actually she's with a pretty tough anti-terrorist bunch, designated Mitzvah Alochaim.'

Jack looked puzzled, 'You'll have to excuse me. My Hebrew is not what it should be. What the hell does that mean?'

'Wrath of God.'

'Right, that's a cool name. So I guess all these party people are with her?'

'Well, they are with her, but until this evening they didn't know her. She's been in deep cover, working in Shahadi's organisation for over a year.'

'Wow,' said Jack, 'but now Shahadi is dead and we have no idea where the plutonium is, we're back to square one.'

'Not strictly true, but I'll let Farida explain all that when we get to Haifa.'

Chapter Seven
'Explanations'

The sun was still to breach the horizon, as the Magma slipped into the port at Haifa. The semi-darkness of predawn exaggerated the blue flashing lights on the waiting ambulances.

With the exception of the medical teams, no other civilians were on the dock. The captain of the Magma supervised the offloading of the wounded. After the ambulances had left the quay, the five hooded prisoners were brought from below deck and secured into two waiting Toyota Landcruisers. Several of the party people escorted the prisoners, while the rest followed in three more unmarked vehicles. Captain Bennie shook hands with Lisa Reynard and Farida Mancini as they left the vessel. On the dock was one remaining Landcruiser.

'That's our ride, Jack,' said Farida.

'Just a second,' said Jack as he took out his smartphone. He checked for a signal and then pressed a speed-dial number.

'Jack?'

'Yeah, hi, Tom.'

'What the fuck's going on, Jack? You okay, mate?'

'Yes, I'm good. I'm in Haifa. I'll give you a bell later; let you know what's happening. I gotta go.'

'Okay. Cheers, Jack. Be safe.'

As the Landcruiser left the dock area, he turned to Farida, 'Where're we going and what happens next?'

'We need to get down to Tel Aviv.'

Jack looked at her for several seconds, 'Listen, I'm not going anywhere until I know who you are and who you're working for, lady.'

'Yeah sure, I guess you deserve some kind of explanation. Let's get some breakfast. It's only about an hour's drive to the city.'

'Some breakfast sounds great, I'm famished,' said Lisa, 'it's been a busy night.'

Farida tapped the driver on the shoulder, 'Take us to the Ben Gurion Hotel, please.'

It was a few minutes before six when they walked into the foyer of the hotel. As they entered the empty dining room a uniformed waitress approached, 'Good morning, table for three?'

They were shown to a window table overlooking the gardens and told by the waitress, 'Please help yourself to the buffet. Can I bring you coffee? Tea?'

'Bring a pot of each please,' said Farida.

They filled their plates with fruit, yoghurt and pastries, then returned to the table. After the waitress had left the hot drinks, Jack turned to Farida, 'Okay, I'm listening.'

She looked at him over the rim of her cup, as she sipped the welcome coffee. 'What has Lisa told you?'

'Only that she's NSA and working with Mossad. Nothing about you. My information was you were Lebanese, so how come you're with Mossad. And how come you knew who I was?'

Farida put down her coffee cup, 'Okay, I'll give you the short version. My father was Italian and my mother was indeed Lebanese. They met in Cairo when he was working there as an engineer. His work then took him to Tel Aviv and my mother, who by then was his wife, went with him. I was born in Tel Aviv. We lived there until I was twenty and then I went to America to study. I came back ten years ago and joined military intelligence.'

'Okay. But what about last night? How did you know who I was?'

'That was me, honey,' said Lisa. A couple of nights ago we were following a guy from Hamas. He met with a European in a bar in the old port. When I saw the surveillance photographs I recognised Tom Hillman. I knew there was a good chance you could be with him and I gave your description to Farida. When a last minute bidder turned up for Shahadi's auction, we expected it to be Tom or you.'

Jack looked at Lisa for several seconds considering what she had just said, then turned to Farida. 'And last night? Other than capturing a few terrorist bagmen, last night served no purpose. You killed Shahadi and the plutonium is still out there. We're back to square one.'

Farida swallowed a mouthful of yogurt and then wiped her lips. 'Last night we took a bunch of terrorist 'bagmen' as you call them, prisoner. They will be interrogated and we will extract information on each of their organisations. We also have sixty millions of their dollars.'

'Err, hold on,' interrupted Jack, 'ten million of that is mine.'

'Yes, of course,' said Farida with a slight smile, 'your money will be returned to you when we get to Tel Aviv.'

'Bloody right it will,' said Jack indignantly, 'but when your assault team took over the Golden Cloud it would have been easy enough for them to get into the secured salon, just blow the doors. But you shot Shahadi. Capturing him would have enabled you to find the plutonium. Why kill him?'

Farida finished her coffee and said, 'Because capturing the man on the boat would have been fruitless. We want the real Shahadi.'

Jack looked at Lisa and then Farida, 'So the guy on the boat was a stand-in, a double?'

'Yes. The man I killed last night was a double.'

'But you do know the real Shahadi?'

'Yes, of course, I've worked with him for more than a year.'

'There's a wider plan, Jack,' said Lisa, 'Last night started a chain of events that would help us recover the material, capture the arms dealer and destroy his organisation completely.'

'We should get going,' said Farida, 'We can fill him in a little more once we get to Tel Aviv.'

Jack shook his head slightly, 'You ladies can fill me in now. Like I said, I'm goin' nowhere until I know the full story.'

Farida looked annoyed and turned to Lisa, 'You tell him. He's beginning to annoy me. But make it quick.'

With a little smile Lisa said, 'He's British sweetie. They annoy everybody.' Then, after taking a drink of coffee continued, 'The set up on the Golden Cloud was to bring out the buyers. We knew there would be several and we wanted to capture them all at the same time. So now we have five 'bagmen' as you call them in custody.'

Jack raised his hand, 'But these guys will be low level in their organisations with a mandate to bid to a certain amount. They're not really anything in the great scheme of things.'

'For God sake, Jack, let her finish,' said Farida.

'Sorry,' said Jack.

Lisa smiled, 'These guys will certainly give us intelligence of some worth. Plus we have their money and their organisations will be pissed about losing that. There's a strong possibility those organisations will think Shahadi conned them just to get the money. They'll probably be planning to take him out as we speak. He'll realise that and will be keeping a very low profile for the time being. He's not gonna expose himself to anyone, not for a while anyway. So the material will stay safely with him.'

'But they could still get to him before we do,' said Jack.

'That's unlikely. They have to find him first. But Farida will contact him and she will be given instructions on where to meet him. Once we finish in Tel Aviv she'll go to him.'

'But how does she keep a valid cover story after last night?'

'One of our team took off in the Golden Cloud's helicopter. Farida will say she took the chopper and escaped before the ship was destroyed.'

Jack smiled and looked at the two women on the other side of the table. The sun was well over the horizon and the early morning in the gardens outside the restaurant was filled with the sound of chirping birds. 'I guess we'd better get a move on then, ladies. Looks like we're all in this together now.'

Chapter Eight
'Room 307'

It was eight thirty when the Landcruiser pulled up to the front of the Tel Aviv Sheraton.

'What're we doing here?' asked Jack, as they entered the cool foyer.

'I'm gonna de-brief and make arrangement to go to Shahadi,' said Farida.

Lisa smiled, 'And I'm going to take a shower and get changed.'

'What? We're not going to Israeli Intelligence?'

'I'm deep cover, Jack. Most of the people in HQ don't know me. And I want to keep it that way.'

'Right. So how long we gonna be here?'

'My handler will be here soon. We could be away in the next couple of hours,' said Farida.

Jack was still wearing the trousers to his evening suit and evening shirt, the jacket had been discarded on the Magma. 'I think I'll see if I can get a change of clothes. I feel a bit Jim Bond-ish in these.'

'There are a couple of nice shops on the mezzanine,' said Lisa, 'Go get yourself something, then come up to the room. It's 307. See you up there.'

Half an hour later Jack took the lift to the third floor. As he walked along the thick carpeted corridor he was greeted by a pleasant chamber-maid who wished him good morning. His knock on the door of 307 was greeted by Lisa's raised voice, 'Come in. It's open.'

The room was large and pleasantly decorated in the usual corporate style for a multi- national hotel chain. The floor to ceiling glass doors opened onto a large balcony that looked out over the sparkling Mediterranean. Lisa stood in front of the windows wearing a white towelling robe, her cellphone to her ear. She indicated for him to take a seat. Instead, he dropped the store bags with his newly purchased clothes onto the couch, found the mini bar and took out a can of Red Bull. As he flipped the ring-pull on the tin, Farida came out from the bathroom, 'You okay, Jack?'

He stared at her for several seconds, the soft drink halfway to his mouth. Her hair was piled up on top of her head and secured with a large pair of designer sunglasses. She wore a black bikini and was in the process of fastening a white, cotton beach robe, when he said, 'Err, yeah. I'm good,' then, realising he was staring, took a gulp of the cold drink, 'I thought you had a de-brief?'

'I'm going to it now,' she slipped her feet into a pair of espadrilles, picked up a small beach bag and a black sun-hat from the bed. At the door she turned, 'See you guys later.'

Lisa was still talking quietly on the cellphone, but waved acknowledgment to Farida as she left the room. Jack looked at the closed door for several seconds then under his breath said, '*What the hell's going on here?*' He took another drink and turned to the American. She still had the phone to her ear as she opened the sliding doors and went out onto the balcony.

'Don't mind me,' he said sarcastically, then finished his drink, picked up the store bags and went into the bathroom.

Jack shaved, showered and changed into the new clothes. By the time he left the bathroom, Lisa had dressed and was sitting out on the balcony. As he joined her she looked over her shoulder, 'Feel better, honey?'

'Yes, I'm good. So what now?'

'Let's go down to the pool and wait for Farida.'

Jack looked at his watch, then took out his cellphone. As he tapped out the text, Lisa caught sight of the recipient.

'Checking in with Nicole, Jack?'

'Yeah, just gonna let her know I'm okay. Right. I'm done. Let's go.'

The Sheraton's pool area was packed with holidaymakers and tourists, and even this early in the morning the bar was busy. Lisa stood and scanned the area, 'I don't see her, let's go out to the beach bar.'

As they entered the private beach area, Lisa saw Farida, 'There she is.'

He looked towards the rows of sun loungers and saw the black floppy hat, 'Yeah, I see her.'

They walked over to the bar, perched up on a couple of high stools and ordered drinks. Lisa's espresso and Jack's water were placed in front of them. From their position they could see Farida clearly and Jack watched as she applied sun protection to her tanned legs. From the corner of his eye he could see the guy coming out of the sea and walking up the beach to the sun loungers. In his mid-forties, he looked very fit, with a deep tan and thick black hair. He stopped at his sunbed, a few feet away from Farida's and picked up a towel. After briefly drying himself, he sat down on the lounger and began flicking through a magazine.

Twenty minutes later Farida stood up, packed her bag, slipped on the cotton robe and walked up the beach, the floppy hat bouncing with each long legged step. She didn't acknowledge her two friends at the bar, but walked straight past, through the pool area into the hotel.

'That's it,' said Lisa, 'let's get back upstairs.'

'What about her bloody de-brief?'

'She just finished it, Jack.'

Chapter Nine
'Leila'

In Beirut, it was a few minutes before nine when Tom Hillman walked into the dining room. He was greeted by a pleasant waitress who smiled and said, 'Good morning, sir. Would you like to eat inside or out?'

Tom looked at the outside veranda and decided it was quieter inside, 'In here's fine, thank you.'

'Please help yourself to the buffet, sir. Can I bring you coffee or tea?'

'Coffee, please. A large pot, I'm expecting a colleague.'

At exactly nine o-clock Akim al Hashem walked into the restaurant accompanied by a twenty-something woman. She wore a pale blue linen dress that did nothing to hide her curvaceous figure. Long dark hair framed a pretty face and her huge dark eyes sparkled under thick lashes.

'Salaam Alaikum, sidi,' said Aki as they shook hands.

Tom moved in close, 'What the fuck is this, Aki?'

The big man smiled and squeezed Tom's hand, 'This is Leila, say hello, give her a kiss and smile.'

Tom did as he was asked. As he kissed the woman's cheek he could smell jasmine. Akim then turned to Leila,

'Darling, would you mind waiting in the foyer, please. I need to talk to my friend in private.'

She smiled, nodded slightly, then turned and left the restaurant.

'Aki, are you stupid? You bring your girlfriend to a meeting.'

'Sit down, Tom.'

Coffee arrived and after the waitress left, Akim said, 'Leila's not my girlfriend. She works for me. She's a hooker and she's here for you. Well, that's what anyone who sees us together will think. She's my cover for this meeting, Tom.'

'What do you mean, she works for you?'

Akim grinned, and leaned across the table, 'I have six girls who work for me. They are providing my pension fund. They also gather information for me.'

'Ah, okay, I understand,' said Tom with a grin, 'Sorry for being so rude. Right my friend, what the hell happened last night at the marina?'

Akim looked serious as he sipped the steaming coffee. 'I'll need a few hours to talk to a couple of contacts. Stay here and I'll be back by three o-clock, four at the latest.'

Tom stood up, 'Okay, let's go.'

They left the restaurant and as they entered the reception area Leila smiled at the approaching men. Akim took her arm gently and returned the smile, 'I'll be back this afternoon, darling.' Then after kissing her cheek turned to Tom, 'Have fun.'

After shaking hands, Tom watched his friend walk out of the hotel, then turned to the woman, 'Okay, this way, Leila.'

Back in his room she dropped her bag onto the couch, 'Akim tells me you are a very special client and I must look after you very well.'

'He did, did he?'

As she started to unzip the back of her dress, Tom said, 'Hold on, love. That's not gonna be necessary. I'm just wanting a little company until Aki gets back.'

'No sex?'

'Not today, sweetie.'

'Oh, okay. But I still get paid?'

'Sure, sure, you'll still get paid.'

She smiled, 'So what will we do until Akim returns?'

'Just relax babe, get some sun on the balcony, or watch TV?'

Leila went to her bag and took out a pack of playing cards. 'Do you play poker?'

'A little, but not very well.'

Her face lit up with a beautiful smile that flashed perfect white teeth, 'Even better. I can win.'

They sat down at the table and Tom watched as she skilfully shuffled the deck. With agile fingers she flicked the cards across the table to him.

'You do that very well, Leila.'

Picking up her cards she smiled again, 'Yeah. I'm a croupier as well.'

Chapter Ten
'Pepsi & Poker'

Jack checked his Rolex. Twenty past ten. The temperature was climbing and the heat hit them as they walked out of the Sheraton and stood under the shade of the elegant portico. Farida handed a small green ticket to the parking valet and the three watched as he scurried off to bring their vehicle.

'It's gonna take us a good six, maybe seven hours to get back to Beirut,' said Jack, just as the valet appeared with a gleaming white Landcruiser.

'We can knock a couple of hours off the journey,' said Farida, 'I know a bit of a short cut.'

Jack smiled as the big 4x4 pulled to a halt in front of them. The oversized tyres and the roof-rack with two spare wheels prompted him, 'We're going off road?'

The valet stepped out and held the door open for Farida. She handed him a tip and he beamed as she climbed into the driver's seat. Lisa quickly moved around the vehicle and climbed into the front passenger seat, as Jack got in the back. As they slowly drove away from the hotel Farida said, 'We'll use the main highway north, but there are a couple of sections where we can go across the desert to speed up the journey. Shahadi's plane will be at the airport to pick me up at five o-clock this afternoon. We should be there in plenty of time.'

They drove in silence as Farida expertly negotiated busy city streets, through the suburbs and out onto the main road towards Lebanon.

'There are drinks in the rear Jack, could you get me one please?' said Farida.

He leaned over the back of the seat and saw two thermal boxes; he was also surprised to see his aluminium briefcase. He picked it up and flipped the lid. Through the rear view mirror Farida smiled and watched as he carefully checked the contents, 'It's all there, Jack.'

He caught her gaze in the mirror and returned the smile, 'Yep, all there, ten mill.'

He reached over the seat, and opened one of the boxes to find bananas, oranges and a plastic bag full of dates. Opening the second he found several bottles of water and a dozen cans of soft drinks. 'Water or Pepsi?'

'Water please,' said Farida.

'Lisa?'

'I'll take a soda, honey.'

He handed over the drinks then took out his cellphone, waited until he had a signal then pressed the speed dial for Tom.

'Jack, are you okay, mate?'

'I'm fine buddy, don't worry. I'll fill you in when I see you later.'

'Where are you now?'

'I'm on my way back to Beirut. Can you arrange a charter jet to be on stand-by for about five o-clock this afternoon?'

'Yeah will do, what's the destination?'

'We don't know yet, probably the Middle East, but who knows, just have the pilot file a provisional flight plan.'

'Will do. Everything else okay?'

'Yes, it's good. Like I said, I'll give you the full story when I see you. Are you okay?'

'Sure. I have my local guy here, out and about asking questions. I'm at the hotel waiting for him to get back to me.'

'Talking of your guy, we need him at the airport as well this afternoon. There's a private jet arriving about seventeen hundred hours. We need the destination of that aircraft before it leaves Beirut. Your guy will have to get hold of the flight plan, so we can follow in ours.'

'Okay, understood.'

'Good. See you this afternoon, Tom. Be safe, buddy.'

'You too, mate.'

They left the suburbs and headed north on the main highway. The road was busy, but Farida pushed on and drove the Landcruiser hard through the local traffic. They had been driving for almost three hours in a north easterly direction when Farida slowed, she pulled the big truck off the road and came to a stop. As they all climbed out she said, 'We'll take a five minute break before we head across the desert.'

Jack stretched the muscles in his back, 'You've gone this way before I guess?

'Yes, a couple of times. It's a bit uncomfortable but saves a lot of miles, and time,' she patted the side of the Landcruiser, 'and in this baby it will be easy.'

Lisa smiled, 'Sounds fun. And we're old hands at desert driving, aren't we, Jack.'

* * *

In his hotel room, Tom was just about to put another twenty dollars into the pot when a sharp rap on the door stopped him. He got up and said, 'Don't touch my cards.'

After checking the spyhole he unlocked the door. Akim entered, 'Salaam, sidi.'

'What have you got for me, Aki.'

'Patience my friend. May I have a drink please?'

'Yes, of course, sorry.'

Tom went to the minibar, as Akim moved over to Leila; bending down he whispered into her ear.

'Nothing. We play poker and I win,' answered the woman, with a huge smile.

'She's a real shark,' said Tom, as he handed his friend the bottle of water, 'I'm over three hundred dollars down.'

'Yes, indeed, my friend,' replied Akim. Then with a salacious wink continued, 'She is very talented.'

'Okay, the game's over, Leila,' said Tom, 'can you wait out on the balcony please?'

Quickly collecting her money and playing cards from the table, she stuffed them into the fake Gucci handbag, then smiled as she made her way to the big glass doors and out onto the balcony. The two men watched her sashay from the room as Akim said, 'You don't know what you missed there, Tom.'

'Oh, I can guess,' he replied with a sigh.

Akim finished his drink, then sat down at the table, 'Last night was very interesting, Tom. My informants tell me it was Mossad that attacked and destroyed Golden Cloud.'

Chapter Eleven
'Departures'

It was almost four thirty when the dust covered Landcruiser pulled up in front of the VIP building of Beirut's Rafic Hariri Airport. They entered the comfortably appointed lounge and were greeted by a young Asian man in smart uniform.

'Good afternoon, madam,' he said to Lisa.

'Hi there.'

Farida stepped forward and took over the conversation, 'I'm Farida Mancini, we are here for a flight at five o-clock.'

'Yes, madam. Your aircraft arrived about two hours ago and is ready for you to board as soon as we process your documents. May I have your passports please? Any luggage?'

'No luggage,' said Farida.

It was only a few short minutes until the Asian returned with their passports, 'Thank you, ladies.'

Farida handed the Landcruiser keys to the attendant, 'Please store our vehicle for me. Someone will collect it in a few days.'

'Certainly, madam, my pleasure,' then, gesturing toward the exit, 'This way please.'

Outside, a large gleaming white Mercedes waited to take them to the flight line; the liveried driver bid them 'Good afternoon,' as he held the rear door open.

Jack had been dropped off at the main entrance to the airport. He'd waited in the shade of a large palm tree and less than ten minutes later the black Range Rover pulled up to the accompaniment of blaring horns from the following cars and taxis. Akim stepped out and made a crude gesture to the waiting cars, as he held open the front door for Jack. The horns continued to blare and as he climbed into the back Akim made another hand gesture to the irate drivers.

As he set off along the airport road Tom introduced the two men, 'Jack, meet my old friend, Akim.'

Jack turned to face the man in the rear, smiled and offered his hand, 'Salaam Alaikum, Akim. I've heard a great deal about you.'

As they shook hands he said, 'Alaikum Salaam, sidi. My close friends call me Aki.'

Jack realised he was staring at the vivid scar down the side of Akim's face, 'Sorry, excuse me, Aki.'

The big man grinned and ran his thumb down the scar from eye to mouth, 'A souvenir from my younger days on the Gaza Strip, Jack. No need to apologise.'

Arriving at the airport they were greeted by the same VIP lounge attendant. After handing over passports, they stood at the big windows and waved goodbye to Akim as he drove away in their vehicle.

'He's done well for us,' said Tom.

'Yes indeed,' said Jack, as the attendant returned.

'Thank you, gentlemen. Do you have any luggage?'

'Just this,' said Jack, holding up the aluminium briefcase.

'May I take that for you, sir?'

'No thank you, it's fine.'

'Very well, if you would kindly follow me, please.'

Another Mercedes was pulling up to the building as they walked out. The driver hurriedly ran around the front of the car and quickly opened the rear door, 'Sorry to keep you waiting gentlemen,' said the driver apologetically.

'No problem, son,' said Jack, as he climbed into the back seat. He turned to Tom, 'So, do we know where we're going?'

Tom grinned, 'Oh, you're gonna love this, mate,' then leaning close to Jack's ear, 'Moscow.'

On board the aircraft Jack fastened his seat belt and looked around the elegant cabin, 'This is very nice. It's the same jet that Dimitri has.'

'That's right, mate,' said Tom, 'was a bit expensive, but the only one available at short notice,' then leaning closer said quietly, 'MI6 will shit, when they get the bill for this.' They both laughed.

The young flight attendant, returned with the drinks they'd ordered and after serving them, said, 'Please let me know if there is anything else you require, gentlemen. Dinner is available whenever you wish.'

Jack smiled, 'Thank you, Stephen. We may eat later.'

The attendant closed the main door and made a performance of ensuring it was secure, then went into the flight deck. A few moments later he returned, followed by the captain.

'Good evening, gentlemen. I'm Captain Caroline Mitchell. Flight time to Moscow will be a little under four hours, but we'll update you once we are at cruising altitude. We'll be clear for take-off in about six minutes. Weather is good for most of the flight, but it may get a little bumpy once we're in Russian airspace. So for now, please sit back and relax. If there's anything we can do to make your flight more comfortable, please don't hesitate to ask.'

'Thank you, Captain,' said Tom.

Jack smiled, 'Yes, thank you, Caroline.'

Jack watched through the window as the small jet picked up speed, then, as if without any effort at all, lifted off the tarmac, banked smoothly to the north and out over the sparkling Mediterranean. A few moments later the discreet seatbelt signs went out and the attendant appeared. 'Can I bring you gentlemen anything?'

'I'll take another beer, please,' said Tom.

Jack raised his hand and shook his head, 'Nothing, thank you, Stephen,' then taking out his smartphone tapped the screen. Several seconds passed and then, 'Mathew?'

'Jack, yes, hello. Are you okay?'

'I'm fine don't worry. Can't talk much over this unsecure connection, but I need you to contact the British Embassy in Moscow.'

'Okay, will do. What do you need?'

'I still have the certificates. I need someone from the embassy to meet us at the VIP Customs area at Sheremetyevo. Tell them to have the documentation for us to clear a brief case through the diplomatic bag, and then hold it for us.'

'Yes, no problem. What's your ETA?'

'Just a second.'

The attendant arrived with Tom's beer, 'Stephen, have we an estimated time of arrival please?'

The attendant placed the drink in front of Tom and said to Jack, 'One moment, sir,' then disappeared into the cockpit. A few seconds later he returned, 'Arrival time at the moment is approximately nine o-clock local time, sir.'

Jack smiled and nodded, then put the phone back to his ear, 'Mathew, twenty one hundred hours.'

'Okay, I'll get onto Moscow now. Anything else? You okay?'

'We're fine. Talk securely later. Cheers, Matt.'

'Take care, Jack.'

Tom took a deep swallow of the ice cold lager and then turned to his friend, 'Right mate, what the hell happened on that ship?'

Chapter Twelve
'Touch Down'

Sheremetyevo is the largest of Moscow's five airports and handles over sixty percent of the international air traffic, so the air space above the huge city is congested to say the least. Flight SK-701-A was in a holding pattern waiting to be given clearance to land. On-board, Farida was impatient to get off, after a flight that seemed to never end. In fact, they had made good time since leaving Beirut and began their decent three and a half hours after departure, but now they were being stacked with the rest of the incoming international flights, awaiting a landing slot.

After circling for almost twenty minutes, Farida's aircraft landed a few minutes before nine. The evening weather in Moscow was pleasant, but being eighteen degrees cooler than Beirut, they both shivered slightly as they disembarked the sleek aircraft.

'We're not dressed for this weather, honey,' said Lisa, as they quickly moved to the waiting limousine.

'We can buy something more suitable,' answered Farida, 'but I'm not sure just how long we'll be here, or where the hell we may have to go next. Shahadi may not even be here.'

The driver wished them each, 'Good evening' as he held open the rear door.

The limousine was warm and after a few minutes drive, they pulled up outside the VIP Arrivals and Immigration area. Once inside they presented their passports to a bespectacled middle-aged lady in a serious looking uniform. After several seconds of scrutinizing and flicking through the pages the woman stamped both passports and handed them back with a curt, 'Spasibo.'

The ladies took the documents, then smiling, Lisa said, 'And thank you too, Ma'am.'

They were then asked by another female uniformed official, if they had any luggage to be inspected, to which they simultaneously replied, 'No.' Departing the official area, they moved into a small Arrivals Hall, where several liveried chauffers were waiting, some holding cards with the names of their expected clients.

'Here,' said Farida, as she moved towards the man holding the *Mancini* card.
The chill evening air hit them again as they exited the building and by the time they had walked to the parked limo they were shivering. The driver quickly opened the rear door and smiled as the two women hurriedly piled into the back. Once in the driver's seat he started the engine and turned the heater up to full. The blast of cool air did nothing to improve the ladies' condition, but a few seconds later the welcome heat came through the vents.

Lisa smiled, 'Oh, that's better.'

'Where are we going?' said Farida.

Looking over his shoulder the driver said, 'Hotel Splendide, Madame.'

'Nice,' said Lisa, then taking out her smartphone, tapped out a short text.

* * *

On board Jack's aircraft, Captain Caroline's voice came over the speaker, 'Gentlemen, Sheremetyevo is particularly busy this evening. We've been advised we are currently seventh to land, which means we should be on the ground in about twelve minutes. I hope you have had a pleasant flight and that your time in Moscow will be safe and enjoyable. Thank you and good eveing.'

'I don't think our time here is gonna be either,' said Tom.

Jack grinned, 'We can but hope, buddy. We can but hope.'

The plane was coming into land, just as his phone beeped. He picked it up and looked at the screen, *Hotel Splendide*. He turned to Tom and showed him the screen.

'So the ladies have landed then.'

As they were leaving the aircraft captain Caroline shook hands and said, 'Good evening, gentlemen.'

'Thank you, Caroline,' said Jack, 'great flight.'

'Thanks,' said Tom, with a smile.

A few feet away from the foot of the steps, the same limousine that had picked up Lisa and Farida half an hour ago waited, its engine running, the driver holding the rear door open.

Jack nodded as he climbed in. 'Thank you,' said Tom as he followed.

Inside the VIP Arrivals building their passports were processed by the same formidable lady who had stamped the ladies' documents earlier. Leaving Immigration, they entered the Customs area and were met by a young man in a smart three piece suit and heavy overcoat. He carried a designer briefcase and smiled as he said, 'Mr Sterling?'

'Yes, hello,' said Jack.

'Toby Gillingham,' said the man as they shook hands.

'How about some ID, please, Toby?'

'Ah yes, of course.' He reached into his inside pocket and produced a small wallet, flipped it open and showed it discreetly to Jack. Under a smart United Kingdom logo and elegantly scripted in English and Russian was written, *Toby Gillingham. Business Liaison. British Embassy.*

Jack smiled at the wording, '*MI6 for sure,*' he thought, 'Thanks, Toby.'

'You need a piece of luggage protecting, sir?'

'Yes, this is it,' said Jack, as he placed the aluminium case on a nearby table.

Gillingham opened his briefcase and removed a large red label on which was written in English and Russian. *British Embassy. Diplomatic Documents.* After sticking the label across Jack's case, he took a document from his own and turned to the waiting Customs Officer. The officer took the document and with an unintelligible comment, waved the three men through to the Arrivals Hall.

'Anything else you need from me, gentlemen?'

Jack handed the aluminium case to the young man, 'Secure this for us please, Toby. Someone will be in touch to recover it.'

'Of course, of course,' then leaning closer to Jack said, 'may I ask what's in it, sir?'

Jack smiled, 'Ten million dollars in bearer bonds. So don't lose it, son.'

They watched as the Embassy man quickly left the building, 'Okay, Tom, you sort us out a car and I'll take a cab to the Splendide. See you at the hotel.'

'See you later, Jack. Be safe.'

Chapter Thirteen
'Hotel Splendide'

The Hotel Splendide stands on the south side of the Moscow Canal and faces the Kremlin and St Basils on the opposite side of the waterway. At over fifty stories high, it is one of the taller buildings in this part of the town, with three hundred and sixty degree views around the city. Built after the fall of the former Soviet Union, it reflects the new attitude to wealth, riches and western capitalism; this place was not for the proletariat.

The limousine pulled up under the brightly lit portico and the driver hurriedly rushed around the front of the car to open the door. He was beaten to it by a smartly dressed valet who bid the ladies, 'Good evening.'

As they left the vehicle, a large man in a dark suit and white open neck shirt came down the marble steps. Farida recognised him as one of the arms dealer's close protection team.

'Hello, Feisal.'

'Good evening. Miss Farida,' said the big man, smiling, 'nice to see you again.'

'Thank you. He's here?'

'Yes, miss. This way please. Mr Shahadi is waiting for you in the penthouse.'

* * *

The huge chandeliers sparkled along the full length of the opulent ballroom. The dance floor was full of elegantly dressed couples; each person wore an ornate mask and danced enthusiastically to the well-known Glen Miller favourite. On stage the thirty five musicians, dressed in bright red jackets performed the old classic perfectly, their flamboyant conductor franticly waving his arms, keeping his band under control and in-time.

Jack had arrived earlier by cab and was already in the bar. Tom had not used the valet service, instead choosing to park the hired Audi R8 a little way from the main hotel entrance, but close for a swift getaway should the situation arise.

Tom joined his friend at the bar, but stood far enough away to give the impression they were not together. The noise of the band covered the sound of their conversation.

'What the hell's all this?' said Tom

'The barman tells me it's a charity ball, arranged by MIDCO.'

'That's one of Shahadi's subsidiaries. Supposed to deal in agricultural equipment, but it's a front company for his arms dealing in the Former Soviet Union states.'

Jack took a sip of his club soda, 'Yeah, he's a clever bastard and well connected here in Moscow.'

'Didn't Dimitri have a deal going with him once?'

'No way. He met Shahadi at some function in St Petersburg. The idiot tried to get Dimitri to invest in some dodgy deal, but Dimitri basically told him to fuck off to his face and pretty much embarrassed the guy in front of a lot of very influential people.'

Tom grinned, 'I guess Dimitri isn't on Shahadi's Christmas list.'

The arrival of the barman interrupted their conversation, 'What can I get you, sir?'

'Just a beer, please,' said Tom. As the barman moved away, he said, 'Where are the ladies?'

'Not sure, but Shahadi, has taken the penthouse, so they must be up there.'

'What's the plan?'

Jack nodded discreetly towards the foyer, 'Let's move out to the reception area. We'll watch the lifts, see who comes down. We need to be sure this is the real Shahadi, if it is, Farida will let us know.'

Chapter Fourteen
'The Penthouse'

Shahadi was sitting behind the mock Louis Quatorze desk when Lisa and Farida entered the penthouse. He did not acknowledge their arrival. He held a large brandy balloon in his hand and was focused on swirling the contents around, enjoying the bouquet that emanated from the amber liquid. He raised the glass to his lips, closed his eyes and took a short sip, simultaneously sucking in a mouthful of air. He made a slight slurping noise as he savoured the taste of the seventy year old cognac on his palette. After swallowing the drink he opened his eyes and looked over the rim of the glass, 'Ah, Farida, my dear. You're here at last. I was so worried about you. I am so happy you are safe, darling.'

Farida, although confident her story wold hold up, was still worried. She knew the man was not stupid, but she counted on his arrogance and her powers of persuasion to convince him she was still loyal.

'Thank you, Vini. I'm perfectly safe now. It was awful; I only managed to get away by sheer luck.'

'And who is this delightful creature with you?'

'This is, Lisa. We're old friends from college, in fact more than that, Vini,' she gave a coy smile and the arms dealer nodded knowingly.

'I ran into her in Beirut a few days before the Golden Cloud meeting. After I got away in the chopper I didn't want to go back to your villa and had to find somewhere safe to go. So I went to Lisa. She's been wonderful. I brought her to meet you, as I hoped you may give her some work with us.'

Shahadi moved from around the desk and took Lisa's hand. He raised it to his lips and said, 'You're very welcome, my dear. We must talk, and see if we can find something for you in our organisation. But that will have to wait. May I get you a drink?'

'No, I'm fine thank you, sir.'

He turned to Farida and smiled, 'Anything for you, darling?'

'Not just now, thank you.'

Shahadi waved his arm to Feisal, 'Wait outside, please.'

Farida took a seat on the elegant couch and Lisa stood next to the open window. The cold breeze coming in off the Moscow Canal refreshed the over-heated room.

Moving over to the well-stocked bar, Shahadi poured himself another cognac, savouring the aroma as the liquid flowed into the glass, 'Seventy years old,' he said, as he turned to the women, 'sure you wouldn't care to join me?'

'I'm sure,' said Farida, smiling.

'No, thank you,' said Lisa, with a slight shake of her head.

For several seconds he looked at Farida in silence, then sat down next to her, 'So, my dear, we had a big problem in Beirut. Please, tell me everything that happened?'

Fifteen minutes later Shahadi stood up and went back to the desk. As he perched on the corner he said, 'You saw the ball down stairs? That event was arranged some time ago with the expectation of celebrating the sale of our special product. But now there is nothing to celebrate. Nothing.'

'If I can . . .'

'Please, darling, I am speaking, you must listen for now.'

'I'm sorry, Vini.'

'Now let me see if I understand it all correctly. My ship was boarded, and attacked by a group, of which we have no knowledge? We have lost sixty million dollars belonging to the key terrorist organisations in the world. We have let their representatives be killed or captured and there is now most likely a fatwah issued against me from these organisations; who probably think I have stolen their money. Not to mention the loss of my beautiful Golden Cloud.'

Farida stood up, 'But . . .'

Shahadi raise his hand, 'Please, sit down. I have not finished.'

Farida smiled, 'Of course. Forgive me.'

'And while all this was going on,' Shahadi pointed a bony finger towards her, 'you, managed to get to one of the helicopters, start up the engines, take off, and escape?'

'Vini, I have . . .'

The man stood up and again raised a hand to silence her. He set the brandy balloon down on a silver coaster, then opened a draw in the side of the ornate desk. The women watched as he took out a small, highly polished mahogany box. After placing it carefully on the desk he opened the lid to reveal a gold plated twenty two calibre revolver. He picked up the gun by the carved ivory handle and gently flicked the cylindrical chamber. The reflected lights sparkled off the gilded weapon, as the finely crafted mechanism spun menacingly.

'My great friend, Colonel Muammar Gaddafi, gave me this. I have yet to fire it.'

Farida looked at him, concern now in her voice, 'I don't understand, Vini. Do you think I have betrayed you?'

The arms dealer said nothing for several seconds, intent on admiring the fine weapon in his hands. 'Do you think I'm stupid, woman? You bring a stranger into my business and tell me she is a long lost lover. That she wants to work with us? This, after what happened on board Golden Cloud?'

'But . . .'

'Shut up,' snarled Shahadi, then turning to Lisa, he raised the gun, 'Who the hell are you working for?'

'What Farida has told you is true, sir. I work for no one. We were lovers in college. We met again in Beirut. I want to be with her and I'm willing to work for you, Mr Shahadi.'

Shahadi smiled and slowly nodded to Lisa, then turned again to Farida. There was no smile in the man's eyes as he pulled the trigger and shot her in the knee.

The sharp crack of the gunshot and the scream from Farida startled Lisa, but it didn't stop her reaction. Survival and adrenalin kicked in and she moved swiftly across the room towards the arms dealer. Farida, her hands holding the smashed bloody kneecap screamed out to her friend, 'No . . .' just as Shahadi spun and fired at point blank range.

The impact of the bullet knocked Lisa backwards onto a small glass table that shattered beneath her. With eyes wide open she stared at the man standing over her. She sucked in a deep breath, grimaced with the excruciating pain, then, as her body went limp, the wide eyes slowly closed.

Shahadi looked at the smoking revolver, smiled, then slowly turned around, 'Now, Miss Farida Mancini, or whatever your name is, you are going to tell me the truth. You are going to tell me everything I want to know, my dear.'

Chapter Fifteen
'Motorway & Murder'

It was almost midnight when the penthouse elevator doors opened and Shahadi and Feisal walked out into the foyer. Jack stood up and cleared his throat loudly, alerting Tom, then inclined his head towards the two men in overcoats and scarves. Tom nodded and watched as they walked to the exit. The bigger of the two went outside, while the tall thin man waited. A few seconds later a long black limousine pulled up and the thin man hurriedly left the hotel and climbed into the back of the vehicle.

'Where are the girls?' said Tom quietly.

'Follow the limo. I'll see what's happened to them.'

Without a word Tom quickly left the foyer and ran to the Audi. He started the engine and with a squeal of the tyres sped after the disappearing limousine.

It had started to rain, but Tom could see the limo two cars in front. The roads were busy, but it was easy to follow the big vehicle through the wide city streets. He knew Moscow reasonably well and from their current direction he deduced Shahadi was heading towards the ring-road that circled the city. As they drove further away from the centre of town the traffic began to thin out, so Tom, with no desire to be detected, dropped back another a couple of cars. They were heading east and within a few more minutes were indeed on the city circular. Shahadi's vehicle picked up speed on the eight lane highway, the rain was heavy now and visibility poor, so Tom had to put his foot down to keep up with the fast moving limousine. It was not long until they passed under the big illuminated sign for Sheremetyevo Airport.

* * *

Jack tried the penthouse elevator, but without a key-card the lift would not function. He quickly moved to the house elevator and impatiently pressed the UP button several times, until the small inverted triangle above the door flashed green. It seemed an age until the doors opened and an older man with two young women in fur coats emerged. The man smiled as Jack entered the lift, the doors closed and he pushed the button for the forty ninth floor. He looked at his reflection in the ornate mirrors that lined the elevator, his mind racing. The lift came to a stop and the doors hissed quietly open. He stepped out into a plush, somewhat over decorated corridor and looked for the stairs. Moving down the hallway he found a door with a sign in Russian and English, *Emergency Exit* He pushed the big handle and waited a moment for any alarms to go off; there was no sound. He quickly ran up the bare concrete steps to the top floor and carefully opened the door to the penthouse level. The corridor was empty and he stood for a second listening. Hearing nothing he moved along the elegant hallway to a large set of double doors. He put his ear to the wood, as he gently tried the handle. He put a hand on each door and pushed; there was movement. He stepped back a couple of paces, took a deep breath, then rushed at the entrance, shattering the silence as he charged in.

The scene in the penthouse shocked Jack for a second. Lisa Reynard was motionless on the floor, surrounded by blood covered shards of glass that glinted like rubies on the pale grey carpet. Farida lay across the couch, her beautiful eyes wide open. The right cheek had been smashed, the bone clearly visible through the once flawless skin. The lower parts of her legs were covered in blood, from the gunshot wounds in both kneecaps. A thin trickle of scarlet seeped from the black hole in her forehead; it ran down the left side of her face, below the open eye, like a crimson tear. Jack had seen dead bodies before, but the pitiful sight of this beautiful young woman's body disturbed him. He stepped forward and gently closed Farida's eyes.

The faint sound behind snapped him out of his reverie and he rushed over to Lisa. Cradling her head he felt for the pulse in the carotid artery. It took a few seconds to find, but it was there, faint, weak, but there.

Chapter Sixteen
'The Clinic'

It was after five in the morning, by the time Toby Gillingham finally got Jack released. As they left the Novodskya Police station, Jack said, 'Which hospital did they take Lisa to?'

'She's in a private clinic, sir. The Pushkin. The police have her under guard and are waiting for her to regain consciousness.'

'Fuck that,' said Jack, 'have you been in touch with her Embassy?'

'Not yet, sir. I've been rather busy freeing you from the clutches of the Russian Police.'

'Get onto the Americans now. She needs to be picked up and taken to their own medical facility. Then meet me at the clinic. What's the address?'

Tom was standing next to the Audi and waved to Jack, as Gillingham walked away.

'Hi, Tom. What's the deal with that bastard Shahadi?'
'I followed him to the airport. He's gone'
'Where's he flying to?'
'We don't know yet, mate.'
'Okay, let's go and see Lisa. The Pushkin Clinic, Severnaya Prospect. It's near the central railway station.'

The two uniformed police officers had no intention of letting the English men anywhere near the woman. They had been told that no one was to go into the side ward, and that's what they would do.

'We're gonna have to wait until the Americans get here,' said Tom.

'I need to speak to her before they arrive. I need to know what happened in the penthouse, what was said.'

'She's still not well enough, Jack. You . . .'

A doctor and nurse arrived and stopped the conversation. Jack pushed past the police officer, 'How is she? Is she going to pull through, doc?'

The doctor looked sheepishly at the police officers.

'Don't worry about them. How is she?'

'Who are you, sir?' said the doctor defensively.

'I'm her husband. Now how the hell is she?'

'We have removed the bullet from her liver. She has lost a great deal of blood. She has several minor contusions on her back, but she is strong and should make a full recover.'

'Can I see her please, doctor? Can I speak to her?'

'You cannot enter,' said the bigger of the two police officers.

'Back off, mate,' said Jack.

Tom put his hand on his friend's shoulder and spoke quietly into his ear, 'Be cool.'

'She's resting now,' said the doctor, 'please, you must let her rest.'

'So she's conscious?'

'Yes, she is conscious. But she's sedated and as I've just said, she needs a great deal of rest. Now please excuse me.'

Jack watched through the window, as the nurse checked the plasma bags. She said something to the doctor who removed a clipboard from the end of the bed. After checking through several pages, the doctor moved to the bedside and held Lisa's wrist. As the doctor checked the pulse, Jack saw Lisa's head move slightly and her eyes slowly open.

Toby Gillingham came through the double doors at the end of the corridor. 'Jack,' said Tom, 'Gillingham's here.'

'Gentlemen, how is she?'

Jack turned, 'Looks like she's awake. I need to get in there and speak to her before the Yanks arrive.'

The Embassy man went over to the police officers, took out his ID and spoke quietly. The huddled conversation started to get a little heated, but after what looked like several threats from the British Embassy official, the bigger of the two officers nodded sheepishly.

'You have two minutes, sir. The officer is calling his superior now to let him know she is awake. So be quick.'

Jack quietly opened the door and went into the side ward, much to the surprise of the doctor.

'I need a couple of minutes with my wife, doctor. Please be so kind as to give us a little privacy.'

'Do not tire her, sir. She is still very weak.'

The small crowd outside the room watched as Jack gently took Lisa's hand, bent down and kissed her forehead.

The corridor doors opened again and two uniformed medics came in pushing a trolley. They were accompanied by two men in dark suits and heavy overcoats.

'Who's in charge here?' the voice was American.

'I am Doctor Vitaly Michkin. How can I help you?'

The American flashed an ID, then handed the doctor a sheet of paper. After reading the document he said, 'I do not suggest she is moved for the moment, sir.'

'She's our problem now, doctor. We'll take care of her.'

The big police officer moved in front of the door and drew his side arm, 'You cannot take her.'

'Stand aside, son. She's an American national and has diplomatic immunity. She's going with us.'

The double doors opened yet again and a tough looking man walked swiftly to the growing group, 'What is going on here?'

The American turned, 'Who are you?'

'I am Senior Detective, Lev Rostov, and this woman is in police custody. She is a material witness in a murder investigation.'

The American handed the document to the policeman, 'You can question her anytime you like detective. Except now. We're taking her to the Embassy's medical facility. Now please have your men stand-aside.'

Rostov folded the document and put it into his pocket, 'Let them go.'

As they watched the ambulance drive away, Tom said, 'This is personal now.'

'No it's not, buddy. I understand your anger, I feel the same, but this is as serious as it gets. We don't know where Shahadi's gone and we've no idea where the bloody plutonium is. We get emotional, we make mistakes.'

'Lisa's our friend, Jack. We take care of our friends. You always said that.'

'She knew what she was doing. They both did. They were agents, it's not our job to look after them. We're after a fucking psychopath who's got a kilo of plutonium. That's the job, Tom, finding Shahadi.'

'Yeah, you're right, mate. Let's get this bastard. Did Lisa manage to give you anything we can use?'

'She was out of it really. But she said something about, *Ras Wasin.*'

'Who's that?'

'I have no idea. But it looks like it's our only lead for the moment. Right now we need to get to the airport and find out where Shahadi's plane went.'

Chapter Seventeen
'Stand-by'

At Sheremetyevo's VIP terminal, Tom had found the supervising dispatcher. It had only taken three hundred dollars to persuade the young man to divulge the destination of Shahadi's aircraft. Jack, in the Audi, was on the phone to Nicole when Tom returned.

'Okay, darling, I gotta go. I love you.'

As Tom got into the warm vehicle he said, 'Bloody hell it's cold here. Either that or we're getting soft.'

'Both I think. How'd you get on? We got a destination for that bastard?'

'His pilot filed a flight plan for Tripoli. Cost me three hundred to get the info. In the old days it would have only been fifty.'

'Yeah, capitalism has replaced communism,' said Jack with a grin, 'I would have thought he'd head back to Beirut though. But then again Farida did tell me he has several rat holes and moves from one to the other regularly.'

Tom nodded, 'Right, he's doing a Yasser Arafat. Never stays in the same place for too long.'

'Okay then, let's go see if we can get a flight to Libya.'

As they were about to leave the car, Jack's mobile beeped. He took out the phone and looked at the display, *MS Calling*. He swiped the screen and said, 'Mathew, hi.'

'Hello, Jack. You ok?

'We're fine, what's up.'

'Are you still in Moscow?'

'Yeah, we're at the airport. We have the destination of the target and we're about to get a flight.'

'Negative, Jack. We need to meet before you pursue the target.'

'What the hell for? We need to get after this bastard.'

'Jack, I've had Tel Aviv and Washington shouting the odds. They are very unhappy that one of their assets has been lost and the other seriously incapacitated.'

'What the fuck, Matt? All the more reason to get after him now.'

'Washington believes our involvement may have contributed to their asset loss. I need you to come back to London and debrief before we make our next move.'

'No way, Mathew. We're going after him '

The phone was silent for several seconds, 'Okay, Jack, forget coming back to London, I'll be on the next flight to Moscow. So do not leave until we meet. Understood?'

Tom looked at his friend and mouthed the words, 'What's going on?'

Jack raised his hand and shook his head, 'Sure, Matt. We'll stand by until you get here. See you in a few hours. Message me your ETA and we'll meet you at the airport.'

Chapter Eighteen
'Ra's Wasin'

One hundred and fifty miles south west of Tripoli are the Ghadamis Mountains. At a height of almost two thousand feet 'Ra's Wasin' is not the tallest mountain in the range, but certainly the most inaccessible. Hence the reason Colonel Muammar Gaddafi built a fortified palace on its peak. The palace, although not especially large, is indeed well protected, as the only access is by cable-car or helicopter.

Following the capture of the terrorist representatives on Golden Cloud, and the subsequent loss of their millions, Shahadi's intelligence network had discovered at least two factions were now seeking retribution and fatwah's had been issued. Although he had several safe locations of his own, he felt the need to take extra precautions. After a short phone call and a payment of twenty million dollars to the Libyan dictator's Zurich bank account, the arms dealer was now safely ensconced in the mountain fortress on Ra's Wasin.

Doctor Grigory Petrov was in his early sixties, a small man with thick grey hair and an equally thick grey moustache. The sparkle of life had left his deep set eyes many years ago and now they peered through rimless glasses that were permanently perched on the end of his thin nose.

Born in Odessa on the northern shore of the Black Sea, his Ukrainian parents had died when he was four. The orphaned boy had been taken to Moscow by Major Vasily Petrov, a Russian KGB officer. The major and his wife had adopted young Grigory and raised him as their own. He'd received an exceptional education and in 1972 had left the Moscow State University with a doctorate in nuclear physics.

Grigory was recruited into the Russian nuclear programme and given work he enjoyed, and excelled at; work that consumed him to the exclusion of all else. There'd been women and lovers in his younger days, but he'd never married, nor did he have any other family. When the Former Soviet Union collapsed, he was dismissed from his position in favour of younger brighter engineers, and suddenly found himself alone and un-wanted.

That was until twenty four hours ago, when the stranger had come to his small apartment in Gorky Prospect. The man had offered him a job, as well as a considerable amount of money. Once he had agreed to take the position, events had moved very swiftly. He'd been taken to the airport, where he'd been treated as a VIP. He'd boarded a private jet, the likes of which he'd never seen before and had travelled in absolute luxury to the Middle East. Now he was in his own suite of rooms in this beautiful mountain-top palace.

The sharp knock on the door made him turn from the window, as a tall slim man entered. 'Good morning, Doctor Petrov. I am Vini Shahadi. I am your host and new employer.'

Grigory offered his hand, 'It is a great pleasure to meet you, sir. I am delighted to be here and have the opportunity to work for you.'

The hand shake was disregarded as a thin smile appeared on Shahadi's lips, 'Good, good. Are you comfortable here, Doctor? Do you have everything you need?'

'Oh yes, sir. It's wonderful. Thank you.'

'Very well, if you will follow me please, I shall show you to your workplace.'

They left the suite and took a small lift down to the sub-basement. Shahadi never spoke until they arrived at the outer door of the laboratory. 'I won't go any further, Doctor. I'm sure you will find everything you need inside. But if there is anything that we have not anticipated please let us know.'

Grigory smiled, a puzzled look on his face, 'Very well, but what is the project? What exactly is it you wish me to do, sir.'

The thin smile crept onto the arms dealer's lips, 'I have acquired a small amount of weapons grade material. I need you to do for me, what you did for your Russian employers, Doctor.'

Petrov removed the spectacles from his nose and looked up into the cold eyes of the man before him, 'You want me to build you a nuclear bomb?'

The thin smile widened as Shahadi placed a bony hand on Grigory's shoulder, 'No, Doctor. I would like you to build me two.'

Chapter Nineteen
'Priviet'

Jack spent several impatient hours waiting for Mathew Sterling's flight to arrive. At a few minutes before six in the evening the Arrivals board declared BA-107 had landed. Twenty minutes later Mathew walked out into the very busy Arrivals area at Sheremetyevo. He could not see Jack or Tom, so took out his phone and was just about to use it when a text message flashed on the screen. *Priviet - end of concourse.*

Mathew quickly made his way down to the end of the packed Arrivals hall and saw the sign, *Priviet* above the entrance to the restaurant. Jack sat at a corner table holding a menu. Tom had taken a seat at the bar and discreetly nodded to the MI6 chief as he entered and walked over to Jack's table. Not wanting to draw attention to their meeting, they didn't shake hands or openly greet each other. Mathew took a seat opposite and picked up the menu, just as a pretty waitress arrived. After ordering, Mathew said, 'How are you, Jack?'

'Okay, we're okay, Matt. You saw Tom at the bar?'

Mathew smiled, 'I did. All very cloak and dagger-ish.'

Their drinks and food arrived and Jack said, 'Hope you're hungry,' as the huge plates of food were placed on the table.

'I ate on the plane. But it'll take a while for us to paw over this; give us time to talk.'

Jack cut the oversized burger in half, took a bite and swallowed the welcome food, realizing he hadn't eaten for over twenty-four hours. 'Okay, boss,' he said, as he washed the food down with the Coke, 'I'm all ears.'

Tom looked at his watch, it had been almost two hours since the de-briefing began. He'd eaten a steak sandwich and drunk three small beers, and was about to order a fourth when the MI6 chief stood up. There was no handshake, but Tom detected a smile from Jack.
Mathew nodded slightly as he left the restaurant, then disappeared into the throng of people in the busy Arrivals Hall. He saw Jack wave the waitress over and pay the bill, then let him get out, before doing the same for his meal. Once they were back in the Audi, Tom said, 'So what's the deal, mate?'

'We're still active. The Yanks have got their knickers in a twist over MI6 getting involved, but Matt has cooled them down. I gave him the full story, right up until this morning. He has no issue with our actions and did point out to the Americans that their agent would be dead if we had not gotten her to a hospital in time.'

'What about, Mossad?'

'Matt said he's still talking to them. Whatever that means?'

'So are we heading to Libya, mate?'

'We are. We need to get on the next scheduled flight to Tripoli.'

'Have we any leads once we get there, Jack?'

'Intel has it, Shahadi has a yacht berthed in Tripoli harbour. He could be there. But we need to be careful; he's big pals with Ghaddafi.'

It was getting dark when Tom returned the Audi to the car-rental company. Jack had gone to check flights for Tripoli and was in the Aeroflot queue when he heard the screams. As he turned, he was hit in the stomach by the butt of an automatic weapon. Winded and gasping for breath, he was thrown to the floor by two large men in full combat gear. Six more stood around him, automatic weapons pointing at his head.

He regained his breath he yelled, 'What the hell is this?'

The two men bound his hands with cable ties. Then, after hauling him to his feet, a man in civilian clothes appeared in front of him.

'Mr Jack Sterling?'

Jack immediately recognised the tough detective from the clinic early in the day, 'Yeah that's me, what the hell's going on?'

The big guys holding him pushed him forward, as the other six heavily armed men cleared a way through the crowd that had gathered. As they hurriedly moved towards the exit the detective said, 'Mr Sterling, you are under arrest for the murder of Farida Mancini and the attempted murder of Lisa Reynard.'

Chapter Twenty
'Banged Up'

Tom was surprised to see two unmarked vans, red and blue lights flashing, parked in front of the departures terminal. He was even more surprised to see his friend being manhandled out of the building. He was only twenty feet away as Jack was unceremoniously thrown into the back of the vehicle, but before the doors closed, they made eye contact and Tom's discreet nod was matched by a slight grin from Jack.

Tom watched as the combat team piled into the vans. Tires screeched and sirens wailed as the small convoy sped out of the airport area.

'What the fuck?' he said out loud. Then took out his smartphone, scrolled down the screen and touched the number for Toby Gillingham.

Over an hour later Tom arrived at Novodskya Police Station. On discovering his passenger was an Englishman, the taxi driver had offered everything from day tours of the city, to hotel accommodation, night club recommendations and hookers. Before getting out Tom paid the sixty five dollar fare with a hundred dollar bill and said, 'Keep the change. If you want to wait, I'll need you shortly.'

A big smile and a thumbs-up from the driver confirmed agreement.

Toby Gillingham was already there when Tom walked into the main waiting area.

'Good evening, sir. I wasn't expecting to see you gentlemen again so soon.'

'Hrrm, yeah, right. What the hell's going on, Toby. I thought you cleared all this up last night?'

'I've spoken to the senior detective and I'm advised they have new evidence.'

'There can't be new evidence. Jack didn't kill anyone.'

'They have him on CCTV coming out of the fire exit on the fiftieth floor. They have him kicking in the doors of the penthouse.'

'That's it? He got there in time to save Lisa's life for fuck sake.'

'Yes, of course.'

'So what happens now?'

'They can hold him for up to seventy two hours for questioning. They'll do a gunshot residue test and run a background check on him.'

'You do realise, Toby, we're working with MI6? If the Embassy here can't get him out and these ridiculous charges dropped, then get the hell onto London.'

'You must understand, sir, the FSB are now involved. They know who you are, and they are, to be crude,

98

pissed off that British agents are running around in Moscow.'

'The Russian Secret Service are just being awkward,' said Tom, with a wave of his hand, 'so you're telling me there's nothing we can do?'

'I'll get the embassy's senior legal officer here first thing in the morning, but I think the best case scenario is he'll be out in seventy two hours, sir.'

'Fuck that,' said Tom as he took out his smartphone.

The phone rang several times before Dimitri answered.

Dimitri Mikhailovich Orlov, was Jack's father-in-law, a billionaire Russian oligarch and the head of a huge multinational organisation. His influence stretched from England to Japan and his network of government and industrialist contacts was legend.

'Tom. Hello there. Is everything alright?'

'Hello, sir. I'm sorry to bother you, but we have a bit of a problem here in Moscow.'

'Tell me?'

Tom quickly went over the events in the Splendide Hotel, leaving out the more sensitive elements.

'So the FSB are now in charge, is that correct?'

'That's correct, Mitri.'

'Okay, give me a few minutes. Where are they holding him?

'Novodskya Police Station.'

'Right, I'll call you back.'

'Err, just one more thing, sir.'

'Yes, Tom?'

'I don't think Jack would want Nicole to worry, so no need to mention it.'

Tom heard a little chuckle, and then, 'Quite right, Tom. Bye for now.'

He re-joined the Embassy man, 'Okay, let's see what Dimitri can do.'

'Dimitri?'

'Dimitri Mikhailovich Orlov. Jack's father-in law.'

'As in, Orlov, the Russian oligarch?'

Tom winked, 'Correct.'

Less than five minutes had passed when his phone beeped, 'Hello, Mitri?'

'Hello again, Tom. He should be released in the next fifteen minutes. If he's not, call me back.'

'Will do. Thank you, sir.'

'Not a problem. You guys be safe.'

Tom smiled at Gillingham, 'He'll be out shortly.'

Chapter Twenty One
'Tel Aviv'

Herzeliya is an upmarket suburb north of Tel Aviv. As well as being the location for many Embassies and Consuls, it is the home of the Israeli Secret Service, Mossad.

In his top floor office Colonel Avi Rishom stood next to the big picture window. From here he could see all the way to the Mediterranean. The knock on the door made him turn, 'Come.'

His secretary entered, 'Excuse me, sir. Danny Shomron is here.'

'Ah, good, thank you, Rachel. Send him in please. And could you bring us some tea?'

'Yes, sir.'

A few seconds later the knock on the door was answered with Rishom's usual, 'Come.'

'Good evening, sir.'

'Hello, Daniel, How are you?'

'I'm good, sir.'

'Really? You're good are you?'

'I'm sorry, Colonel. I meant I was okay. Of course I'm not good. Not with the death of Farida Mancini.'

The knock on the door broke the tension as the tea was brought in.

'We'll help ourselves, thank you, Rachel.'

'Yes, sir.'

The colonel picked up the tea pot and as he poured, said, 'Tea, Daniel?'

Shomrom was still bristling from his boss's comment, 'No thank you, colonel.'

'Sit down, my boy. Have some tea. I believe you had become quite close to Farida?'

'Sir?'

'Daniel, I'm the head of Mossad, you think you could hide something like that from me?'

'Yes, sir, we were. Very close.'

As the colonel passed the cup, he said, 'I have read your report on the current status of the Shahadi operation. I was never that keen on having to work with our cousins from Langley, but needs must. How is their agent by the way?'

'Lisa Reynard, sir. She's still in their Moscow embassy. Quite poorly. They plan to get her back to Washington as soon as she's strong enough to travel.'

'Good, good. I'm pleased she will pull through.'

'Yes, sir. Me too.'

'So, Daniel, how would you like to take over the Shahadi operation yourself? I know you have other business you are currently overseeing, but I think we can cover that.'

Shomron took a sip of tea, his eyes narrowed and he looked at his boss, 'Yes, colonel. I would. Thank you, sir.'

'The recovery of the plutonium must remain number one priority, you understand?'

'Yes, of course, sir.'

'But I think we can dispense with any idea of capturing Mr Shahadi, I will leave his demise entirely up to you my boy.'

Chapter Twenty Two
'The Metropolitan'

It was not fifteen minutes, but twelve, since Tom had taken the call from Dimitri. Jack came out from the interrogation area with a stern face, Detective Lev Rostov following. As he collected his personal effects from the desk sergeant, Rostov said, 'Mr Sterling, or whatever your name is. I suggest you leave Moscow as soon as possible. I think you have overstayed your welcome,' then with a slight smile, 'at least for this visit anyway.'

Jack grinned and held out his hand, 'No hard feelings, detective?'

As they shook hands the Russian said, 'No hard feelings. Dasvidanya.'

As they left the police station Toby Gillingham said, 'May I drop you gentlemen anywhere? The airport perhaps?'

Jack grinned, 'Tom, it sounds like we're not welcome. Looks like everyone wants us outta town.'

'Doesn't it just? I wonder why?'

Jack looked at his Rolex, 'It's almost midnight. Let's get a hotel and have a decent sleep. We can sort out flights tomorrow.'

'Never mind sleep,' said, Tom, 'I could do with a decent drink.'

'A drink it is then, buddy. Toby, would you care to join us for a night cap, son?'

'I'll take a rain check, gentlemen,' then after shaking hands, walked down the steps. At the bottom he turned and said, 'Please try and stay out of trouble.'

The taxi driver was out of his cab when he saw Tom, 'You need ride now, boss?'

'Yes, we need ride now, mate. Where too, Jack?'

'How about the Metropolitan Hotel?'

'Okay, good choice,' said the smiling cabbie, 'Metropolitan have great nightclub.'

It had started to rain as the taxi pulled up in front of the Metropolitan. Tom paid and generously tipped the driver, who continued his marketing, 'Thank you, boss. You sure you no need ladies?'

Jack laughed at the Russian's fractured English, 'No, we no need ladies.'

The foyer was busy, but there was no one waiting at the Reception desk. The pretty girl smiled welcomingly as they approached, 'Good evening, gentlemen.'

Jack smiled, 'Hi there, we need a couple of rooms for tonight please. We don't have reservations'

'Just a moment, sir,'

Tom looked around and said quietly, 'This place is jumping eh?'

'Yeah, looks prety busy.'

'I have two rooms' sir. One on the ninth and one on the tenth floor.'

Jack handed over his passport and credit card, 'That's fine, thank you.'

'Any luggage, sir?'

Jack smiled and shook his head, as the girl handed back the card.

'Do you need the porter to show you to your rooms?'

'No thanks, we're gonna have a nightcap.'

'Very well. Enjoy your stay, gentlemen.'

Jack smiled, nodded, then turned to Tom, 'Bar or nightclub?'

'We should just have a quiet drink in the bar, but fuck it, nightclub.'

They took the stairs down to the basement club and were greeted by a heavily built Russian in evening dress. He nodded towards a small pay-booth where the girl at the desk smiled and said, 'Twenty five dollars each, please.'

Tom took out his wallet and handed over the money, as the girl passed him two tickets. The music hit them as the big Russian opened the door. The place was classy with what appeared to be an upmarket clientele. The main room was on two levels with a circular dance floor in the centre and a raised seating area surrounding it.

Several smaller VIP booths were accessible from the raised area and all looked to be occupied. The music was not current, but the rhythm and beat had the dance floor full of party-goers. There were two bars, one which appeared to be only servicing the long legged, big boobed waitresses and the other for customers. Tom pushed his way through the crowd and up the steps to the punters' bar. Two high stools had become vacant, thanks to the eviction of a couple of drunk young men who were being unceremoniously escorted out. Moving quickly to the bar, Tom beat two other guys to the stools.

The barmaid smiled, 'What can I get you, sir?'

'Coke and a large beer, please,' said Tom.

Jack sat down and dropped a twenty dollar bill on the counter. The barmaid returned, put the drinks down and picked up the twenty, 'Another five dollars please, sir.'

Jack handed her a ten saying, 'Keep the change, love.'

It was difficult to hold a conversation, so they watched the dancers and enjoyed the music.

Tom was ordering a second round, when Jack tapped his back and leaned close to his ear, 'It's pretty dark in here, but I'm sure we know this guy?'

Tom paid for the drinks and turned around, 'Who?'

'Left of the service bar, second booth along. Big guy in the leather jacket, sitting with two blondes.'

Tom took a swig of beer as he looked towards the booth, 'Bloody hell, Jack. It's Bogdan Markov.'

They moved around the raised seating area towards Markov's booth. He was far too busy with his face sunk into the ample bosom of one of the blondes, to notice them arrive at his table. The blonde whose bosom was being worshipped, pulled the big man's head from her cleavage and nodded to the two strangers. Markov looked at the men, then stood up, put his hand under his jacket and pulled out a large pistol. The blonde screamed as he pointed it straight at Jack. Tom and Jack slowly raised their hands. Then the big Russian burst out laughing.

Chapter Twenty Three
'2am Sauna'

Bogdan Markov was in his late fifties, a big man with a cheerful face that belied his tough character. In his younger days he'd been a helicopter pilot with the Spetznaz, the Russian Special Forces. Jack had first met him in Kosovo after he'd left the Soviet military. Bogdan was working as a mercenary and had secured himself a lucrative contract as a mountain guide working for the United Nations. Markov had joined Jack's team for a covert mission on the Kosovo border that resulted in the neutralisation of a particularly nasty Armenian warlord. Although they had only seen each other a dozen times since then, the three men had become great friends.

The Russian put the gun back under his jacket and almost knocked the table over as he lumbered past to embrace his friends. As he bear-hugged them both, Tom said, 'Bloody hell, big man, let's get a breath, mate.'

'What the fuck you guys doin here?'

As he was released from the Russian's grip, Jack said, 'We had a bit of business.'

Bogdan's face screwed up, and he shook his head. Then tapping his ear, 'Can't hear very good. No good to talk here.'

Jack leaned closer and said, 'Let's go upstairs to the bar?'

Markov leaned forward and indicated to the two blondes behind, 'We going for banya, I meet you in the Spa. Twenty minutes, da?'

Jack looked at Tom, 'You fancy a sauna at two-o-clock in the morning?'

'What the hell, okay.'

Jack nodded and gave a thumbs-up as the big Russian sat down between the two ladies.

The temperature gauge read sixty five degrees. 'This is the first time I've been warm since we got here,' said Tom.

'It's all that Dubai living, buddy. It's making you soft.' Jack stood up and re-adjusted the towel around his waist as Bogdan entered the sauna, followed by the two women. The Russian turned to his companions, pointed to a platform in the corner and as the girls walked away patted them on their backsides.

'Is very good to see you again, my friends,'

'You too, Bogdan, you've lost some weight, buddy,' said Jack, as he slapped him on the shoulder. Jack looked at the tattoos on the big man's arms, old military insignia and mottos in Russian Cyrillic. But on his chest were two newish works. On the left, over his heart, was an ornate Orthodox crucifix and on the right, a beautiful depiction of St Basil's Cathedral. The tattoos that drew his attention though, were the stars on each knee. 'What's this?' said Jack tapping the man's left knee. You're working for the Mafia now?'

Bogdan turned and said, 'You know the marks, my friend?'

'I do. Stars mean Mafia and stars on the knee means, *You Bend The Knee To No Man.*'

The big man grinned, 'Times are hard, Jack. We get older, is more difficult to find good paying work. And there are no more honourable wars to fight. Just the terrorist bastards.'

'What happened to the Kazakhstan gig, Bogdan?' said Tom, 'I heard you were head of security for a Kazakh oil company?'

'Da, my friend, but the bloody Kazakhs got upset when a helicopter went missing.'

'It crashed?' said Jack.

'Niet. It went missing!'

Jack and Tom both laughed. 'Who did you sell it to, Bogdan?'

'My cousin in the Ukraine has crop-spraying business. I make him good price for the chopper. But not possible for me to go to Kazakhstan now, so I join the wild bunch here in Moscow. But I also have couple of things on side. Have a few girls working for me and I have nightclub downstairs.'

'The club is yours?'

'Da, it was crazy place before. Drug dealers, prostitutes, much fighting. Was real shit hole, so I make deal with hotel. I clean place up and lease from them. Now is high class place, with good customers, no drugs, no fighting,' then with a wink and a grin, 'still a few hookers though.'

'That's great, Bogdan,' said Jack, 'so I guess you wouldn't be interested in a little work with us?'

The big Russian turned to Jack, 'Anytime with you guys, I am interested, my friend.'

'Okay, then we'll see you in the morning. How about midday? Meet in the bar here?'

'Midday for sure,' then pointing to the two half naked blondes, 'You guys want these two? No charge. On the house. '

Jack laughed, 'We're good thanks, buddy. You have fun.'

Chapter Twenty Four
'Bad News'

It had rained heavily all night, but by midday the weather had changed and a watery sun was appearing through the clearing clouds. Jack had not slept well and had gone down for breakfast just after seven-o-clock. He'd been seated at a window table and was enjoying the hustle and bustle of the busy Moscow street when the waitress brought him the second pot of tea. He'd finished his breakfast half an hour ago and was pouring his forth cup as Tom entered the dining room.

'Morning, buddy.'

'Jack, where's your phone?'

'What? I gave it to the concierge to charge up. Why?'

'They've been trying to get hold of you. They just called me. Hold on, I'll do call-back.'

Tom passed the phone to Jack. Three rings later a woman's voice said, 'Tom?'

'No this is Jack. Who's this?'

'Jack, oh thank God. This is Isabelle, Nicole's PA.'

'Hello, Isabelle, what's going on?'

'There's been an accident, Jack. Nicole's in hospital.'

He stood up and looked out the window, 'What's happened to her?'

'We were at a charity event last night. We were driving home. We were crossing on a green light, when this other car appeared from nowhere. It ran the red and ploughed right into the side of us.'

Jack took a deep breath; he could feel his heart pounding as he cleared his throat, 'My wife, Isabelle. How is my wife?'

'Nicole will be okay, Jack. She has a dislocated shoulder and a broken wrist. She has a few minor cuts from the glass, but the air-bag saved her.'

'Oh, Jesus. Thank God,' he coughed and cleared his throat, 'and you, you're okay, Isabelle?'

'I'm fine, Jack, some bruised knees. But there's something else.'

'What?' there was silence on the other end of the line, 'what else, Isabelle?'

'They think she has lost the baby, Jack.'

'What baby?'

'Oh, Jack, I'm sorry, I thought you knew.'

'Is she able to speak now?'

'No, they've sedated her.'

'Okay, when she comes round tell her I'm on my way back. I'll be there soon. Which hospital is it?'

'Saint Bart's'

'Thank you, Isabelle.' He handed the phone back to Tom, 'You heard that?'

'Most of it, mate, yes. Is she okay?'

'She's okay, but she was pregnant. And I didn't know.'

Jack looked at his Rolex, it was almost seven forty five, 'I need to get back, Tom.'

'Of course you do, mate.'

'But what about the job?'

'Go'n see Nicole, stay as long as you need, then catch me up. Catch us up, if we get Bogdan on board.'

'Right, yeah. Can you check flights to London? I'm gonna make a couple of calls.'

They left the restaurant and went down to the foyer area. It was busy with tourists and guests checking out. The concierge had a couple of people waiting, but Jack jumped the queue, 'I'm sorry, I have an emergency call I need to make,' then turning to the concierge recovered his fully charged phone.

Tom was busy scrolling through flights on his phone when Bogdan appeared, 'Good morning, Tom.'

'Bogdan, morning, I didn't expect to see you until noon.'

'Is Jack about yet?'

Tom pointed to his friend over by the concierge, 'He has a family emergency.'

'What's happened?'

Tom raised his hand, 'Just a second, mate. I'm trying to sort out a flight for him to London.'

Jack was waiting for the line to connect, then a couple of seconds later heard, 'Jack, hello. You okay?'

'Hi, Mathew. Yeah, I'm fine. But Nikki's been in an accident. I need to get back to see her.'

'Is she okay?'

'She's had a car accident. It doesn't seem to be that serious, but she's in Saint Bart's. Could you go see her, let her know I'm on my way, please?'

'What are you doing for a flight?'

'Tom's on that now.'

'Okay, soon as you have an ETA let me know. I'll have someone pick you up.'

'Thanks, Matt. See you later today.'

Jack joined his two friends, and as he shook hands said, 'Good morning, Bogdan.'

'Morning, boss. Sorry to hear about your wife.'

'Cheers, buddy. Any luck with a flight, Tom?'

Tom held up his hand, then continued to tap away at his smartphone screen, 'Right, I've reserved a seat on the eleven-thirty from Sheremetyevo to Gatwick. We need to leave now and get you to the airport. You can pick up the ticket at the BA desk.'

'Great. Let's get a cab. Bogdan can come with us, we can talk on the way.'

'Fuck taxi, I drive you. We get there faster.'

The Russian's driving was not only embarrassing, but downright dangerous. The big Ford Ranger truck was an imposing vehicle, but driven by Bogdan it was a lethal weapon. He disregarded the speed limit, weaved in and out of lanes, flashed lights, beeped the horn and cursed at anything that did not get out of his way.

'Calm down, big man,' said Tom, 'we're okay for time. Let's get to the airport in one piece, mate.'

'Airport road will be busy, my friends. Need to make good time now, just in case.'

Jack laughed, 'It's your licence, up to you if you lose it.'

The Russian winked and laughed, 'No problem. I just get another one.'

Jack leaned over from the back seat and put his hand on Bogdan's shoulder, 'Okay, we need to tell you what we're doing. Well, the broad strokes first. Then if you're in, we can tell you the full story.'

'Just tell me full story, boss. Whatever it is, I'm in for sure.'

The next half hour was spent with Jack outlining the mission, reiterating events on the Golden Cloud and the recent actions of the arms dealer in the Splendide Hotel. They were approaching the airport as he said, 'You sure you want in, buddy?'

'I have heard of this Shahadi. He is ruthless man. It will be a pleasure to help you.'

'Good, we're lucky to have met up with you, Bogdan, especially now as I need to get back to London.'

'For me it is honour to work with you guys again.'

The big vehicle pulled into the carpark and the three piled out, Tom said, 'Once you're away, we'll sort out flights to Libya.'

'Yeah, you and the big man get down there and see what you can find out. Soon as I know how Nicole is I'll be in touch. I'll be back as soon as I can.'

'Take all the time you need, mate. Give her my love.'

Jack embraced Tom and then the Russian, 'You guys be safe down there. I'll see you in Tripoli.'

'Da,' said Bogdan, a huge grin on his face, 'Dasvidanya.'

Chapter Twenty Five
'Bombs, Bullets & Business Class'

The business class cabin was full. Jack took his seat as the attendant arrived with a tray of drinks, 'Water, orange, Champagne, sir?

'A coke when you have time please?'

'Certainly, sir.'

He strapped himself in, took out his smartphone and tapped out a text, *BA808, ETA Gatwick 12:00.* He looked out the window and watched as the luggage truck backed away. His thoughts of Nicole were interrupted as the attendant returned, 'Your coke, sir.'

'Thank you, we gonna get away on-time?'

'Yes, sir. We should be on our way in about ten minutes.'

An hour later the flight attendant tapped Jack on the shoulder, 'Sorry to wake you, sir. Will you be taking lunch?'

'It's okay, I wasn't sleeping. Err no, I don't think I want anything thank you, just some tea, please.'

'Certainly, sir.'

He had adjusted the time difference on his watch when he'd boarded the aircraft and the Rolex now showed ten thirty five, '*Ninety minutes to London,*' he thought. He took out the smartphone and checked emails and messages. The first message from Mathew confirmed he was with Nicole and she was okay. The second said someone would pick him up at Gatwick.

The attendant arrived with his tea, 'Anything else, sir?'

'No, thank you.' Slipping on the headphones, he settled down to watch a movie.

* * *

Tom had found there were only three flights a week to Tripoli and although his last minute booking seemed like it would miss the cut-off point, the nice lady behind the Aeroflot desk had managed to give him two seats on that afternoon's flight. Tom smiled as he took back his credit card and picked up the tickets, 'You need to go back and get your passport. I'll wait here for you.'

The cheery Russian's face lit up as he pulled out a leather travel wallet from his inside pocket. He flipped it open to reveal his documents, 'I have several passports, boss, and I travel all the time. This one I keep in the truck.'

Tom laughed, 'Yeah, of course you do. The old rules are the best rules. *Always be ready to move at a moment's notice*. Okay, we got five hours to kill. Not much point driving back to the city and then back here.

What you say we go for a long lunch at the Airport Hilton?'

'Da, good idea.'

'And you can tell me all about the mischief you've been up to since we last met?'

In the Hilton, Tom had spent several frustrating minutes on his smartphone, searching for, and eventually booking, a decent hotel in Tripoli. They'd eaten a pleasant lunch, after which, Bogdan had entertained with stories of his exploits over the last couple of years. But it was how he had been seconded into the notorious Moscow Mafia that surprised Tom most.

'It was when I first take over club. The place was packed and many villains in this night. There is big argument in one VIP booth. I go to see problem and this guy is yelling at Vanya Kuragin . . .'

'The mafia boss?'

'Niet, that is Alexei Kuragin, this was his son, Vanya.'

'Ah, okay.'

'So like I say, there is big argument. Is about some woman I think, not sure. But is getting pretty bad and I'm with my guys trying to calm situation. So things calm down and the guy is walking away, he's swearing and still angry, but he's walking away. So my guys leave and I turn to go. Then is scream. I turn round and this fucking idiot has gun pointing at Vanya. So I rush him

121

just as he pulls trigger,' Bogdan raised his glass and took a long drink.

'So what happened? Did he shoot Kuragin?'

'Niet. The bastard shoots me when I jump in front. I stop Kuragin getting shot.'

'Were you, okay?'

As he tapped his upper arm the big Russian smiled, 'Da, nine millimetre in my shoulder is nothing. I knock this idiot to ground and Vanya's men take him out of club. I go to hospital and am okay. Next day two men come to club, say Mr Alexei Kuragin want to see me.'

'The mafia boss?'

'Da, the big chief. So I go to big house in Leninsky Prospect, and he is there with his son Vanya. We drink vodka and he tells me I have saved life of son. Says he is in my debt, I say is no problem, is my pleasure. He asks how my wound is, I tell him is okay. We have more vodka and soon he asks if I want to work with him.'

'And you obviously said yes?'

'Da. So I have job protecting Vanya for a few months, and make some good money and fix up club. Now I only work on special jobs for Mr Alexei. Is good story eh?'

Tom laughed, then took a drink, 'Da, Bogdan, is good story.'

* * *

Doctor Grigory Petrov had been working constantly and by eating and sleeping in the laboratory, he was well ahead of the schedule required by Shahadi. The huge bonus he had been promised was too good to miss and he would do all possible to have the work finished before, or at least, on-time.

He was working on the final assembly of the second device when the intercom startled him, 'Excuse me, Doctor. Mr Shahadi sends his compliments and asks if you would care to have dinner with him this evening?'

He put down the micrometer and pressed the intercom button. 'Yes, of course, Please tell Mr Shahadi I would be delighted to.'

'Thank you, Doctor.'

Chapter Twenty Six
'Fast Ride to St Bart's'

At twelve-fifteen local time, BA808 bounced onto the tarmac at Gatwick and by twelve thirty-five Jack hurried out of the double doors and into the busy Arrivals area. Quickly scanning the waiting crowd, he saw the young woman dressed in a tight leather motorcycle suit, holding the placard with his name.

'Hello there,' he said, pointing to the card,' That's me.'

'Good afternoon, sir. I'm told you would have no luggage?'

'That's correct.'

'Okay, this way please. I'm to get you to Saint Bartholomew's as quickly as possible.' The girl pushed her way through the crowd and once outside said, 'We're just at the taxi rank sir.'

As they approached the waiting line of cabs, Jack smiled for the first time since hearing news of the accident. Standing next to a powerful BMW motorcycle was a heavily armed airport policeman. As the pair approached, the girl said, 'Thank you, officer.'

'You're welcome, miss. Ride safe.'

Jack nodded to the departing cop as he took a helmet from the girl, 'I'm impressed.'

'You okay on the back of this, sir?'

'I haven't ridden since I was a kid.'

'Just hold on tight,' she smiled, 'we won't be observing any speed limits.'

The thirty-eight mile journey from Gatwick to Saint Bartholomew's would normally have taken at least an hour and forty minutes by car. Precisely thirty five minutes after leaving the airport, the BMW pulled up in front of the hospital entrance.

Jack climbed off the bike and removed the helmet, just as a parking warden arrived, 'No stoppin' 'ere. Move it.'

The girl quickly pulled off her helmet, set it down on the fuel tank, and unzipped a pocket in the sleeve of her jacket. She took out a small wallet and flashed the ID. The official looked at it, shook his head, then walked away with an unintelligible grunt.

'That was some ride,' said Jack, as held out his hand, 'I'm sorry, I never asked your name?'

The girl took off her right glove and shook hands, 'Victoria, sir.'

Jack nodded and smiled, 'Thank you, Victoria.'

'You're welcome, sir. I hope everything will be okay in there.'

Mathew Sterling was in the corridor as Jack came through the door, 'Jack, good to see you.'

As they hugged Jack said, 'Good to see you too, bro. Where is she?'

'In here.'

Quietly, he pushed open the door and entered the side ward. Nicole was sitting up in bed, a plaster cast on her hand and wrist, her arm in a sling. There were several small cuts on the right side of her face, a couple of which had butterfly stitches, 'Zaikin,' she said, delightedly.

'Oh, my darling, what've you been up to?' He leaned down, took her face gently in his hands and softly kissed her lips. 'How're you feeling?'

'Shoulder is a bit sore and my wrist hurts a lot, but apart from that I feel fine.'

He sat down next to the bed. A tear trickled down his cheek, 'I was so worried about you, baby.'

Nicole smiled and brushed the tear from his face, 'Talking of babies.'

'I know, darling. Isabelle told me you lost it. I didn't know you were pregnant, I . . .'

'Jack, shhhh. They only said they *thought* I had lost it. I didn't. You're going to be a father, Zaikin.'

Chapter Twenty Seven
'Uncle Mathew'

Although the rear of the plane was packed, Tom was surprised to see how few passengers were occupying the business class cabin, so the flight, although bumpy at times, had been reasonably comfortable and the service and food, surprisingly good. At the Hilton, Bogdan had drunk a lot more than he should, resulting in him falling asleep before the seat belt signs were switched off. Tom had never been to Libya before and although he knew much about the dictator and his regime, he knew little of the country, other than its ability to produce a lot of oil. He spent most of the flight on his smartphone, referencing as much as he could of the geography and infrastructure of this North African country. The departure from Moscow had been delayed for over an hour, so it was almost ten o-clock in the evening by the time Aeroflot 701 landed at Tripoli International Airport.

It had taken them almost an hour to get through Immigration and then a further fifteen minutes were spent explaining to a very suspicious Customs Officer why they had no luggage. Once outside, the temperature made Tom feel more comfortable than he had been for several days, whereas the big Russian was not at all happy with the heat.

'Fuck, it's hot, boss.'

Tom laughed and slapped his friend on the back, 'It's almost midnight, Bogdan, and this is night-time temperature. Wait till the morning, mate.'

They made their way to the taxi rank and joined the long queue. Tom watched as the battered old cabs arrived, picked up their fares and drove off to the accompaniment of backfires, rattles and diesel smoke. After a further ten minutes they were at the front of the queue and reluctantly climbed into an old Mercedes. Unfortunately the air-conditioning was non-existent, but the lack of a rear windscreen helped with ventilation. The driver mumbled something in Arabic and Tom said, 'Corinthia Hotel.'

* * *

Nicole's room was warm and somewhat stuffy and the dozen or so flower arrangements made the place seem even more claustrophobic. Jack took her hand and kissed the back of it, 'Why didn't you tell me you were pregnant, darling?'

'I wasn't sure. I wanted to have a check-up before I said anything. They say I'm just over ten weeks, so it's early days.'

'This is wonderful, Nikki. I love you, baby.'

There was a knock on the door and Mathew entered, 'Okay if I come in?'

Nicole smiled, 'Of course.'

'Now that you two lovebirds are together, I need to get back to work. Sorry.' Mathew kissed her on the forehead, 'Get well soon, gorgeous. Jack, can I have a quick word, please?'

The two men left the room, 'I'm so pleased she is going to be okay, Jack, and I believe congratulations are in order.'

Jack smiled, 'Yes, you're gonna be 'Uncle Mathew' in a few months.'

'I can't wait and I'm very happy for you. Okay, on to more unpleasant things. What's the situation with our friend Mr S?'

'Tom is on his way to Libya as we speak. We met an old friend of ours in Moscow. He's been seconded into the team. Quite fortuitous, considering I needed to get back here.'

The MI6 chief frowned, 'Who's the old friend?'

'Bogdan Markov, ex Spetznaz, ex mercenary, working with the Moscow mafia now.'

'Oh, what wonderful credentials. Sounds an ideal addition to your little band.'

Jack grinned, 'No need for sarcasm, brother. He's a capable guy, he's loyal and trustworthy.'

'Jack, I trust your judgment. If Mr Markov is an asset, so be it.'

'Bye the way, Matt, I need some equipment before I go back.'

'Sure, whatever you want. Right, I must get over to Vauxhall Cross. Call me in the morning about the equipment and let me know when you plan to leave.'

'Okay, thanks, Matt.'

'Congratulations again, daddy.'

Jack grinned.

Chapter Twenty Eight
'Reminds me of Saddam's place'

The Corinthian used to be one of the top hotels in Libya, in fact it was the only true five-star in the country. Recent events, and rumblings of dissent amongst the population, together with the instability of the regime, were now impacting on the number of foreign businesses coming to the North African oil producer. The mood in the country was uneasy to say the least and the dictator's ruthless treatment of his subjects did nothing to improve the situation.

The battered old Mercedes miraculously arrived at the front of the hotel. Almost by way of complaint it backfired emitting a noxious black cloud of diesel smoke. The surly driver, who had said nothing the whole journey, beamed when Tom paid the fare in hard currency.

Although the hotel was imposing on the outside, the interior brought visitors down to earth with a bump. The welcome from the man behind the receptionist desk was curt and suspicious. Tom handed over his passport and credit card, then looked around the once magnificent foyer, 'Reminds me of one of Saddam's palaces.'

Bogdan grinned, 'Is okay. I been in worse places.'

'Yeah, you're right. Me too.'

The man behind the desk handed back his passport and card, 'No luggage?'

'No, mate. We travel light.'

The receptionist tapped an ornate bell and an old man came from the back office, 'Rooms five-o-five and five-o-six.'

The old man took the keys and smiled when he saw the guest were foreigners. Still smiling he pointed to the lifts, then hurriedly limped towards them. They rode to the fifth floor in silence, the elevator rattled to a stop and the doors hissed open. The porter moved in front of them and stopped at the first room, unlocked the door and handed Tom the key. Tom nodded a thank-you and gave the old boy a ten dollar bill, which resulted in the man kissing the back of Tom's hand. Before entering his room he looked at his watch, 'It's well after midnight, mate. Let's get some sleep. Meet for breakfast at nine o-clock?'

'Okay, boss. See you in morning.'

At Bogdan's room, the old porter unlocked the door and stood back, a beaming smile on his weathered face, unfortunately this was only rewarded with a grunted, 'spasibo,' from the Russian.

* * *

Nicole had been seen by the doctor and after a short visit from the gynaecologist, was discharged just after seven in the evening. Not wanting to drive all the way out to their Berkshire home, Jack had asked Isabelle to take them to their London apartment in Maida Vale.

'Are you hungry, baby?'

'Not really, but tea would be nice. Actually I'd love a glass of champagne to celebrate, but that's off limits now.'

'Yes. No booze for you, young lady. I'll run a bath for you and bring your tea in.'

'That would be lovely, darling.'

'Oh, bugger, I said I'd let Tom know you're okay. He sends his love by the way.'

'Call him now then.'

Jack looked at his Rolex, 'It's well after midnight in Libya, I'll leave it until morning.'

'Libya? I thought you guys were in Beirut?'

'That was two countries ago, Nikki. I'll tell you all about it when you're in the bath.'

Chapter Twenty Nine
'Breakfast & Brothels'

The once elegant restaurant in the Corinthian was now looking decidedly shabby, but the breakfast buffet was passable with lots of fresh fruit, yogurts, warm bread, and a large fresh honeycomb dripping with golden liquid. To the side was a grill area where a reasonably clean chef was cooking eggs and omelettes to order. Tom was piling bacon and scrambled egg onto a chipped plate, when Bogdan arrived. 'Morning, boss. Sleep well?'

'Morning, mate. Yeah, I did.'

'Da, me too. Food looks good, but what's this shit?'

'Your guess is as good as mine. I only eat what I can recognise.'

'So what's the plan?'

Tom winked, 'Get some breakfast and we'll make one.'

A waiter, in a white jacket that had seen better days, brought a steaming jug of coffee to their table, as Bogdan sat down with a plate stacked with sausages, eggs and bread.

'Bon appetite,' said Tom.

Picking up a fat sausage, the big Russian grinned, 'Nazdorovia.'

By the end of breakfast, and a second pot of coffee, they had formulated a plan, largely based on what Jack and Tom had discussed in Moscow. Tom would check out the marina first, to see if the arms dealer's yacht was still there. Bogdan would concentrate on the cafes and illegal brothels around the dock area, for information from the less desirable elements in the city.

'All we need is a lead on Shahadi's whereabouts. Ask questions discreetly. Don't make a big deal of any information. Jack got a name from Lisa Reynard, *Ras Wasin*. See if you can find out anything about him? Okay, my old mate, you had enough to eat?'

'Da, let's go.'

As they walked to the foyer Tom's smartphone beeped, 'Jack, good morning. How's Nicole?'

'Morning, buddy. Nikki's fine, thanks. She's back home now. Got a cast on the wrist and a few cuts, but nothing that won't heal. And the better news is, she didn't lose the baby.'

'Jack, that's terrific, mate. Congratulations.'

'How you guys doing down there?'

'We're staying at The Corinthian. Just heading out now to see what intel we can pick up on Mr. S.'

'Okay, good. How's our Russian friend?'

'Sober and full of food, so good to go,' Tom heard Jack laughing, 'let us know when you're coming back?'

'Will do. Nikki's fine now she's home. If I can get her to take a few days off work, I'll be down there, the day after tomorrow.'

'Cool. Okay gotta go, taxis are here. Love to Nicole.'

'You be safe, Tom.'

'Always.'

The day had been exceptionally hot and without the usual breeze from the Mediterranean the humidity was high. By six in the evening, Bogdan was ready for a shower and a cold drink, and not necessarily in that order. Tom had got back to the Corinthian an hour or so earlier and was in the bar talking on his phone when the big Russian entered.

He ordered a cold beer from the barman and joined Tom. 'Okay, boss? You look worried.'

'That was my contact in Beirut. He has some information for me.'

'Da? What was it?'

'He wouldn't say over an unsecure line. Wants to meet back in Beirut.'

'You better get your ass over there then.'

The barman arrived with the drink, 'You want anything, boss?'

'No thanks, mate. I'm okay for now.' He watched as his friend finished half the beer and then leaned across the table, 'So how'd you get on today? I was all over the marina and there is no sign of Shahadi's boat.'

The Russian finished off the rest of the beer and waved at the barman for another, 'I did okay.'

'Good, what you got?'

'I go to couple of cafes on docks, found one with brothel upstairs. Has four girls from Ukraine, nice girls, friendly,' the Russian gave a salacious wink, 'they tell me about one guy from big ship in the dock. This guy is engineer, a Frenchman. He is part of crew on ship that belongs to MIDCO or MIDCOM company?'

'MIDCO is one of Shahadi's companies.'

'Okay, but the girls tell me, this Frenchman says there is two ships for MIDCO.'

'Two ships? But I checked the whole marina. I never even saw one that could have been Shahadi's'

'Not marina, boss. The docks.'

The second beer arrived and Bogdan sipped at the foam, 'This French guy tells girls he works for big business man called Shahadi. He boasts about what a big shot his boss is.'

'That's great information, mate.'

'Da, is good. So I go see if I can find the boats, but this part of dock is secure. No chance to get in. There is many military and naval ships.'

'Could you hire a small boat and check it out from the seaward side?'

'Sure, is easy.'

'Okay, tomorrow I'll get up to Beirut and you go and have a look at this naval dockyard. Great work, Bogdan, great work. Right, let's get something to eat.'

'One more thing, boss. This *Ras Wasin* guy. Is not a guy, is a mountain.'

'What?'

'Da. I talk to one guy in café. He tells me *Ras Wasin* is mountain in south of Libya.'

Tom stopped and looked at Bogdan's smiling face, 'A mountain?'

'Da. A mountain.'

Chapter Thirty
'Good Morning'

Jack hadn't slept at all. The bath had relaxed Nikki and when they'd eventually got to bed, she had quickly fallen asleep on his chest. He'd held her in his arms all night, listening to her breathing and feeling her warm body next to him. He never thought he could love her more, but now with a baby on its way, the feelings of love for this beautiful woman were almost overwhelming.

His smartphone buzzed quietly. He leaned over as carefully as he could and picked it up from the bedside table. *TH Calling*, showed on the screen. Almost in a whisper, he said, 'Hi, Tom.'

'Jack, sorry to disturb you so early. How's Nicole?'

'She'll be okay. Whatsup?'

'I had a worrying call from Akim al Hashem, in Beirut. Says he needs to talk to me face to face. Said it's very important.'

'Can you give me a few minutes, buddy and I'll call you back?'

'Okay, mate.'

Nicole rolled over, and in a sleepy husky voice said, 'Good morning.'

He leaned down and kissed her gently, 'Sorry, baby. Didn't mean to wake you.'

'Mmmm . . . it's okay.'

'I need to talk to Tom, go back to sleep.'

He pulled the sheet over her, slid out of bed, and went into the drawing room. He tapped Tom's speed-dial number and waited.

'Jack?'

'Yeah, okay tell me again, buddy.'

'Like I said. Aki seemed very worried and was clearly not happy about having to call me.'

'So what's your plan?'

'No choice. I have to get back to Beirut. It's obviously something big if he wants to meet in person.'

'Yeah, your right. Look, I'll spend the day with Nikki and get the first flight down to Tripoli in the morning. You go see your pal Akim.'

'Yes, I plan to get a flight today and be back tomorrow morning, maybe tonight?'

'Cool, stay in touch. Be safe.'

'Cheers, mate.'

As he put the phone down Nicole came in, 'Everything okay?'

'Yes, just talking to Tom.'

She stood against him, stroked his cheek, then put her good arm around his neck, she looked into his eyes, and kissed him, 'Good morning, again.'

Chapter Thirty One
'Two Clouds'

Bogdan had chartered a small motor boat and hired fishing tackle from an old man on the quayside. He knew he'd paid more than he should, but did not want to attract unnecessary attention by getting into a haggling situation with the old Lebanese.

By late-afternoon he'd sailed from the fishing harbour, past the private marina and down the coast to the naval dockyard. Dropping anchor about half a mile from the mouth of the docks he could see most of the vessels that were berthed. He used the powerful field glasses he'd brought, and scanned the small fleet of ships that constituted Gadhafi's navy.

At first he didn't see the white yacht moored behind the coastguard cutter, but after moving his tiny craft fifty yards to the east, the beautiful seagoing ship came fully into view. Adjusting the binoculars, he read the name on the stern, *Golden Cloud 2*. The ship berthed alongside was identical, the name on the stern, *Golden Cloud 3*. He took out his smartphone and zoomed in with the camera feature. After taking several pictures, he checked the photos and was happy they showed both yachts clearly. He tapped out a message and attached the photos, then pressed send.

In London, Jack's phone beeped. He swiped the screen, and smiled, 'Nice one, Bogdan.'

* * *

It was early evening and the sun was setting over Beirut's old port area, when Tom entered the café. He'd looked around the dimly lit room, fully expecting Akim to be there. The place was quiet with only a couple of drunks at the bar and another two men playing dominos in the corner. He took his usual booth at the back, as the waiter arrived, 'Water, please. Leave the top on.'

The waiter grunted and walked away, as Tom took out his phone. He tapped out a short message, *Here Now.*

The grunting waiter returned and placed the water on the table. Tom's phone rang and he quickly checked the screen, fully expecting it to be Akim. The screen said, *Bogdan.* He opened the message and smiled when he saw the photos of Shahadi's twin yachts.

The seedy café was starting to get busy with locals, sailors and the odd tourist. Tom opened his second bottle of water, and then checked his phone for the third time. Nothing from Aki. The time display read, 20:37, over two hours since he'd arrived.

Soraya el Hashem had been married to Akim for over twenty five years and in all that time she'd never been in a café or bar. As she stood outside The Old Turk, she trembled a little at the thought of being in such a place. She wrapped her hijab tightly round her head and face, took a deep breath and with shoulders back and head high she entered the smokey establishment. Even after all these years she still recognised Tom Hillman sitting in the corner booth. As she walked to the back of the darkened room, she ignored the crude remarks of the two drunks at the bar. She stopped at Tom's table and for a second she could see he was surprised, until she dropped the hijab from her face.

'Soraya, what the . . .? What're you doing here? Please, sit down.'

'Salaam, Tom. It has been many years since we have met. You do not look any different.'

He remembered the pregnant woman he'd helped to escape the apartment building all those years ago. The woman across the table from him had matured, but the years had been kind and she was still as attractive as she had been then, except for the deep dark circles below her bloodshot eyes.

'Soraya, it's good to see you, but you shouldn't be here. Where's Akim?'

He watched as the tears welled up in her eyes. She looked around the room, then reached into her pocket, took out an envelope and slid it across the table. She eased back into the shadow of the booth, sniffed and wiped the tears from her cheeks, as Tom opened the letter.

Tom, my good friend.

If you are reading this, then I am dead.
I hope this letter gets to you in time, to stop what could happen.
Shahadi as you know planned to sell the raw plutonium to the highest bidder; the attack on Golden Cloud stopped that plan and caused him a serious problem with the organisations involved. He has become the target of a unilateral fatwah and to escape this, he has a new plan. He has manufactured two nuclear bombs and has promised the organisations, that he will explode one bomb in Tel Aviv and the other in New York.
For this to happen they will pay him collectively two billion dollars. Hamas, Hezbollah, Al Qaeda, the PLO and ISIL, will each pay four hundred million.
Unfortunately I cannot give you any information on his whereabouts, only that he could be in Libya. I cannot help you find him. That is now up to you and Jack.

I think I told you once why I joined Hamas. To fight for my people, not to murder millions of innocents. So you must stop this madman.
One last thing I ask of you, Tom. Get my family to safety. Please get them out of Lebanon.

Allah be with you my friend.
Aki . . .

Chapter Thirty Two
'Thank You, Doctor'

The huge balcony looked out over the Ghadamis Mountains. Vini Shahadi was sitting at a lavishly laid breakfast table when Grigory Petrov arrived.

'Good morning, my dear Doctor.'

'Good morning, sir.'

'Come, please sit down and join me.'

'Thank you, sir. That's very kind.'

'Not at all. I must say I enjoyed our chat over dinner the other evening. Interesting your adoptive father being in the former KGB. I, myself, have several friends in the old regime.'

Petrov smiled, not understanding where the conversation was going, until Feisal appeared with a large leather briefcase.

'And now you have finished your work, Grigory.'

'Yes, sir. And as instructed I have briefed Mr. Feisal on the arming procedure.'

The thin smile appeared, 'Excellent, excellent. So, now we come to your remuneration,' the arms dealer nodded, and the big bodyguard placed the case on the table.

With the smile still present, Shahadi pointed to the case, 'Please, Doctor.'

Petrov stood up and flipped the locks. His eyes widened and he too smiled.

'Three million dollars, as agreed. Plus another two for meeting our stringent deadline. You may count it if you wish.'

The three men laughed as the case was closed. Shahadi wiped his hands on his napkin and stood up, 'Feisal?'

The big man took out an envelope and handed it to the old Russian, 'A little extra something for you, Doctor.'

Inside the envelope was a first class air ticket to Moscow.

'Thank you, sir, for everything. If I can help again in the future I'd be pleased to do so?'

'Yes, indeed, we may well call on your expertise again. Now if you will excuse me, I have a lot of work to do. Feisal will accompany you safely to Tripoli.'

Petrov held out his hand, but no handshake was given, 'Goodbye, sir.'

The cable-car lurched, as it pulled away from the dock and began the slow decent down the side of the mountain. Petrov stood at the panoramic windows enjoying the magnificent view as the swaying car trundled its way downwards. His thoughts turned to the money in the case, and how it would change his life; he could do so many things now. Perhaps go to . . .

He didn't feel the blow that broke his neck. The car creaked and swayed violently when Feisal pressed the emergency stop. He steadied himself and waited for the movement to subside, then carefully opened the door. Taking hold of the legs, he dragged the body across the floor, and then pushed it out into the hot Libyan air. He watched, fascinated, as the corpse spiralled and then smashed into the jagged rocks below. He closed the door, picked up the case and hit the start button. By the time he'd arrived at the top, the vultures were already fighting over the carcass of Grigory Petrov.

Chapter Thirty Three
'Back at the Corinthian'

The chauffeur arrived just after seven. Nicole travelled to Heathrow with Jack, and the two of them waited together until the 'last call' for boarding was announced. He'd kissed her and held her gently in his arms until she said, 'Okay, time to go, darling.'

'Yeah. I'm sorry, baby, but it's very important. You know that?'

'Of course. I'm fine. Dad arrives today from Japan, so I'll have him fussing over me. Now go and do what you have to, and come back safely.'

'I'll call you when I arrive. I love you, Nicole.'

She smiled and touched his cheek, 'I love you too. Now hurry.'

Jack's plane touched down in Tripoli at six-thirty local time. Tom arrived from Beirut an hour earlier and was waiting in the busy Arrivals area. Bogdan was in the Short Stay parking, in the old Land Rover he'd bought that morning.

Tom waved to Jack and they eased their way out of the busy Arrivals Hall, and then out past the throng of travellers fighting for taxis. The rear door of the Land Rover was open, and Bogdan stood on the open tailgate.

He waved as he saw his friends emerge from the crowd milling around the exit.

As they approached, the smiling Russian said, 'Welcome back, guys.'

They shook hands and Jack looked at the battered vehicle, 'Nice motor.'

Tom grinned, 'We needed something discreet to get around in.'

'Fair enough. Does it go?'

'Da, is not too good outside or inside, but engine is okay.'

'Great, let's get out of this heat and back to the hotel then.'

The big Russian frowned, 'Might not be able to do that, boss'

'What? No hotel?'

'Hotel is ok,' he shrugged his shoulders, 'but no air-con in jeep.'

A small dust covered Fiat 500, the engine running, was stopped next to the car park exit. As the Land Rover drove past, the Fiat pulled out and quickly fell in behind the battered old vehicle. Bogdan was out of the airport area and onto the main city road within minutes, the little Fiat following, three cars behind.

Back at the Corinthian, Jack checked in, the old porter appeared, smiled, and limped his way to the lift. After the porter had unlocked the door, Jack handed him a five dollar bill, resulting in the hand kissing, from the delighted old man. Inside, Bogdan opened the mini-bar fridge but found it empty. He went to the phone and dialled room service, 'What you want to drink, boss? There's nothing in fridge.'

Jack took out his smartphone, 'Get them to send up some beers, cokes and water, please, big man,' then hit the speed-dial for Nicole. The phone rang twice, 'Zaikin, you okay?'

'Hi, babe. Yeah, fine, landed safe and back at the hotel with the guys. How are you feeling?'

'A lot better, I might go into the office tomorrow.'

'Well, if you feel up to it. I have to go, babe, talk soon.'

'Okay, take care, daddy. I love you.'

Bogdan answered the knock on the door. The waiter came in and put the drinks down, Jack quickly signed the bill and handed the guy five dollars. Beers and coke were cracked open and the three men sat down.

'Right, gentlemen. You've been busy while I was away. Tell me what you've got?'

An hour and four beers later, Jack stood up, 'Tom, I'm so sorry for your friend Akim. Any idea what happened?'

'His wife Soraya said she found him in front of their house. His throat had been cut.'

Jack opened another can of coke, 'We don't know who did it?'

Tom shook his head, 'Could've been Mossad? More likely his own people, if they'd found out he'd been talking to me?'

'We'll do the right thing by his family. Get them out to Jordan, or the Emirates, where ever they want.'

The room was silent for several seconds, then Bogdan said, 'What about the engineer?'

'We need to question him soon as possible. Can you get your Ukrainian lady-friends to let us know when he shows up at the brothel?'

'Sure, boss. They say he's there every night.'

Tom laughed, 'The dirty bastard.'

Jack grinned, 'He's French. Right, big man, get down there now and set it up with the girls,'

'Okay, boss.'

As he was leaving the room, Tom said, 'Make sure you pay them enough to keep their mouths shut.'

The Russian grinned, 'Niet, problem.'

A few minutes before ten, Jack's smartphone beeped, the message from Bogdan read, *Frenchman is here.* He turned to Tom, 'Let's go.'

Chapter Thirty Four
'The Frenchman'

The taxi dropped them in the old town, dock area. As Tom paid the cab, Jack looked up and down the quayside. About fifty yards away, parked next to a couple of trucks, stood Bogdan's Land Rover. The place was starting to get busy with the seedier element of the city coming out to play, or conduct business. Prostitutes, drug dealers and punters mingled together along the gaudily illuminated promenade. They passed several cafes, each one with a man outside, touting for their business. Across from the Land Rover, a flickering neon sign above the entrance read, *Café Negro*, and below a smaller sign blinked, *Massage Ici*.

Inside, Bogdan was waiting at the end of the bar. He nodded as his friends entered the smoke-filled café and then turned towards a red velvet curtain at the back of the room, he pulled it aside and opened the door.

Jack looked at Tom, 'Lovely place.'

Tom grinned, 'It has a certain charm.'

They eased their way past the busy bar area, through the curtained door and followed the Russian up a dimly lit staircase. On the landing, they were greeted by a pretty girl who was clearly pleased to see the big man again. She put her finger to her lips and pointed to a door at the end of the hallway. Bogdan patted her on the backside, and made his way to the end of the corridor. He turned the handle quietly, opened the door slowly, then burst into the room. The naked Frenchman yelled at the sudden intrusion, jumping from the bed when he saw the three men. His hands covered his subsiding erection then his anger and indignation turned to fear, 'Que diable est-ce?'

Tom picked up the man's trousers and threw them at him, 'Coitus interruptus, mate. Get your pants on.'

The girl on the bed stood up and slowly put on a silk robe, clearly comfortable being naked in a room full of men. Bogdan went over and whispered in her ear, which brought a smile to her pretty face. She leaned up and kissed his cheek then left the room.

They manhandled the struggling engineer down the stairs and through the rear door into a small garage. Bogdan pulled over an old wooden crate and pushed the Frenchman down. Tom looked at the man for several seconds, 'What's your name, mate?'

'Marcel Dubois. What the hell do you want?'

'Okay, Marcel, we just need some information. If you answer our questions, no harm will come to you. If not, my friend *Mr B* here is gonna practice his dentistry skills on you.'

Bogdan picked up a pair of pliers from the workbench and waved them in front of the man's face.

'Mon Dieu, non. Je vais vous dire . . .'

'In English, Marcel.'

'Oui, I mean yes. Anything you wish to know, I will tell you.'

Tom took a bottle of water from his pocket and handed it to the shaking man, 'There are two yachts in the dock, both named, Golden Cloud.'

'Yes, yes. Two in the dock here and the first Golden Cloud is in Beirut.'

Jack smiled, 'Not anymore.'

'Monsieur?'

Jack shook his head, 'Nothing, Marcel,' then turning to Tom, said, 'Carry on, *Mr T.*'

Tom placed a hand on the man's shoulder, 'And which ship do you work on?'

'*Golden Cloud 3,*' he took a gulp of water, 'I am chief engineer.'

'You know the owner of these ships?'

'Oui, yes, of course. Monsieur Shahadi.'

'Is he on board?'

'No, we have not seen him for many days.'

'Do you know where he is?'

The engineer smiled nervously, 'No, monsieur,'

Bogdan pushed Tom out of the way, 'Liar,' he screamed as he gripped the Frenchman's jaw, the open pliers inches away from the man's trembling lips.

'Please, monsieur, please. I swear it is the truth.'

The grinning Russian stood back, 'I think he tells truth, boss.'

Tom looked at Jack and shook his head, 'Take it easy, *Mr B*. Okay, Marcel, just breathe. You're doing well.'

The man finished the water as tears appeared in his eyes, 'I will help you. I have said this.'

Jack stepped forward, 'Does your boss have any property here? A villa, a house, apartment?'

'No, I don't think so. He usually stays on board. But the helicopter pilot told me he had taken Monsieur Shahadi to a place called, Ras Wasin.'

Tom nodded to Bogdan, 'Keep an eye on him.'

Jack moved away from the engineer, and whispered, 'He's in Gadhafi's stronghold, on the bloody mountain.'

They returned to the Frenchman and Jack leaned in close to the man's sweaty face, 'How much do you earn in a year, Marcel?'

'Monsieur?'

'How much money do you earn in a year?'

'Two hundred thousand, dollars.'

'How would you like to earn a year's salary, Marcel?'

The engineer looked puzzled, then the slightest of smiles appeared, 'Oui, of course.'

Twenty minutes later the Frenchman hurriedly left Café Negro, but not before Jack had paid him three thousand dollars, 'This is by way of compensation for interrupting your evening's enjoyment, Marcel. If you do what we want, you'll be well rewarded.'

'Oui, monsieur. For two hundred thousand, I will be happy to help you.'

Bogdan had left next. He drove to the end of the quay, parked, and with the engine running, waited for his two companions to follow. It was almost eleven thirty when the battered Land Rover, with its three occupants departed the old town area. As they discussed the evening's events, none of them noticed the little Fiat 500 following them.

The Corinthian bar was quiet, with only a handful of businessmen sitting around talking. They ordered steak sandwiches, beers and tea, then, at a corner table settled down to formulate the next day's plan.

'We need to get on board those ships, and as the engineer can only get us one security pass, then it's gonna have to be you, Tom.'

Tom nodded, 'No problem. The Geiger-counter you brought back is easy for me to conceal.'

'Good, be careful eh?'

Jack took a bite of his sandwich and washed it down with a mouthful of tea, 'Okay, Bogdan, you and I'll sort out a light aircraft and take a little flight down country to the Ghadamis Mountains. The GPS on the satellite phone picks them up nicely, so let's go have a look at this Ras Wasin.'

'Okay, boss.'

'Did you manage to get hold of any weapons?'

Bogdan smiled, 'Da, I buy two automatics, and one short barrel shotgun. I hide them in back of truck. Also have plenty ammunition for all guns.'

'Good job, big man. Let's hope we don't need them.'

'Right,' said Tom, 'if that's it, I'm off to bed. Eight o-clock for breakfast?'

Jack nodded, 'Sounds good.'

The garden and pool area were in darkness. The man watching from the shadows saw the three get up and leave the bar. He moved out of the bushes and made his way back to the vehicle parked on the approach road. Once inside, he tapped out a text message, waited several seconds, then smiled as he read the reply. As the Fiat 500 drove away, the man behind the wheel began to whistle.

Chapter Thirty Five
'Charlie Mike, Nine-Five'

Bogdan pulled up a hundred yards away from the entrance to the naval dock yard. As Tom left the vehicle he turned, 'You guys have a safe trip.'

Jack smiled and gave a thumbs up, 'Be careful, buddy. We can't trust the Frenchman.'

'Yeah, no problem.'

Bogdan grinned, 'Tell him I fix his teeth if he tries to fuck us.'

Tom shook his head, and walked across the road to the small news-stand. He picked up a paper and handed the old vendor a few coins, then waited for the engineer to arrive.

Bogdan looked at his watch, 'He's late, boss,'

Jack smiled, and then pointed to the security gate, 'Look.'

Marcel Dubois flashed his ID to the gate guard as he left the secure area. He wore white trousers, and a crisp white shirt. The ornate epaulettes on his shoulders glinted in the morning sun, and with his officer's cap set rakishly over his left eye, he looked every bit the suave man of the sea, until he saw Tom at the news-stand.

In the old Land Rover the big Russian grinned, 'Aww, he is so cute.'

Jack chuckled, 'Isn't he just.'

Tom folded the paper and smiled, 'Bonjour, Marcel.'

The engineer looked nervous, but appeared less afraid than the night before, 'Bonjour.'

'Okay, so you can sign me into the dock yard, yes?'

'Yes, no problem. I have told the captain you are an old friend and I am giving you a tour of the yacht.'

Tom put the newspaper back on the counter, and turned to Dubois, 'Okay. Let's do it.'

Jack watched as the two men walked away, 'Right, buddy, time to go.'

Bogdan started the engine, did a three point turn and set off for the airport.

The Fiat 500's air-conditioning was turned up full, but it was still too warm for comfort. The man behind the wheel spoke into his smartphone, 'One has gone into the dock yard, the other two are leaving,' he lowered his head as the Land Rover drove past, 'No, sir. Yes, sir. Yes, I'll follow the vehicle.'

The roads were busy with trucks, cars, buses, and the occasional donkey cart. Jack could see the frustration on his friend's face, and grinned as the big Russian cursed at every vehicle on the road. Never-the-less, he was surprised to see Bogdan maintain his composure and drive as un-aggressively as he could.

It was late morning when the Land Rover drove into the outside parking of the old civilian airport. 'We'll leave the car here,' said Jack, 'We can't show up in this. They'd never charter us a plane.'

Bogdan looked offended, 'This is great car, boss. British made.'

'Yes, mate, but it's a fucking heap.'

The young man at the charter office was surprised when the two men walked in. The instances of someone hiring a light aircraft were now few and far between, so he was delighted when he discovered they were Westerners.

'Good morning, gentlemen. My name is Yossi, how may I help you?'

'Morning. We'd like to charter the twin engine Cessna. What's the rate?'

'Certainly, sir. It's five hundred dollars an hour, plus one thousand a day insurance.'

'We'll need it for about four hours.'

'May I see your PPL, sir?'

'I don't have my Private Pilot's Licence with me, but . . .' Jack took out a thick wad of five hundred dollar bills. He handed the man six, 'That's for the hire and insurance,' then he counted out another ten notes, 'and five thousand more for you.'

'Oh, that will do nicely, sir. But I still need some identification.'

Jack handed the man his passport, 'This do?'

Yossi flipped open the document, 'Thank you, err, Mr. Sterling. We'll hold onto this until you return, sir.'

'Certainly,' said Jack, smiling.

The heat was building and the sun was now high in the sky. Out on the flight-line Bogdan was sweating as he watched Jack conduct the pre-flight checks. The exterior of the small aircraft was carefully inspected, then Yossi opened a concealed valve under the wing. He ran a few centilitres of aviation fuel into a Perspex container and dropped a small white lozenge into the liquid. Jack watched and waited a few seconds, and nodded, 'Okay, the fuel's pure. Thank you, Yossi.'

Jack and Bogdan climbed into the compact cabin and strapped in. They put on head-phones and Jack took out the pilot's check list. The big Russian waited patiently as his friend went through the procedure. A few minutes later Jack said, 'Right, let's go.'

Yossi stood in front of the aircraft and gave a thumbs-up as the two engines were fired into life. He waved, and stepped aside, as Jack skilfully taxied away from the flight line and out onto the runway.

'Tower control, this is Charlie Mike, Nine-Five, ready for take-off.'

The radio was quiet for a second or two, then a static filled voice crackled, 'Roger, Charlie Mike, Nine-Five. Clear on runway one.'

'Thank you, tower.'

Bogdan watched as his friend eased the throttles to fifty percent. The brake was released and the aircraft began its run along the tarmac. As the speed increased Jack pushed the throttles to maximum, pulled back on the column and smiled as the aircraft rose gracefully into the blue Libyan sky.

Chapter Thirty Six
'In-coming'

At the naval yard security gate, Tom was signed in by Dubois. The docks were busy with a high presence of uniformed naval personnel and civilian contractors. The main area housed what constituted the Libyan Navy, further out to the seaward end of the facility were several private yachts belonging to Gadhafi and his closest friends. It was here, Tom expected to see *Golden Cloud 2* and *3*. 'Where's the other one?'

'Monsieur?'

'Shahadi had two yachts here. Where's the second one?'

'*Golden Cloud 2,* set sail during the night. But my ship is exactly the same.'

'I wanted to check over both vessels, Marcel.'

'I'm sorry, monsieur; I did not know it was leaving.'

'Was Shahadi on board? Do you know the destination?'

'I cannot say. I have nothing to do with *GC2*.'

'Shit. Okay, let's look over this one.'

On board *Golden Cloud 3*, Tom was introduced to the captain and first officer, Dubois had then conducted the tour of the main decks, staterooms, galley and crew's quarters. They were now in the engineer's office. Tom had discreetly checked the Geiger-counter in each location and although there were trace reading, the highest pulse came from the engine room.

'There is nothing radioactive on the ship, monsieur.'

'We'll see wont we?'

The Frenchman shrugged, 'Oui, monsieur. As you wish.'

'Anything out of the ordinary happened lately?'

'Monsieur?'

'Strangers? Unusual cargo? Anything odd?'

'There are always strangers. Monsieur Shahadi entertains a many people. He always has guests. But since we have been in Tripoli, there has been no one that I know of.'

'What about the yachts? Are they always berthed in here?'

'No, this is the first time we have been here together. But we have been told we will be leaving soon.'

'Oh, yeah? When?'

'We have orders to be sea-worthy at all times and be ready to leave at a moment's notice.'

'Right. What about destinations?'

'No destination has been advised, monsieur.'

Tom stood up and looked through the office window at the huge diesel engines, 'What's the range of one of these things?'

'Fully fuelled, we have a maximum range of four thousand five hundred nautical miles.'

Tom turned to Dubois, 'Really? That far?'

'As long as we run at optimum speed, yes.'

'And what would be the optimum speed?'

'Forty knots is sustainable with these engines.'

'Hrrmm. Okay. And you have no idea where the other ship is heading?'

'No, monsieur, I swear.'

* * *

The flight south had been smooth enough and the tail wind from the north had made the journey shorter than expected. Jack checked the satellite phone's GPS and the compass bearing on the control panel, 'Ghadamis Mountains, dead ahead.'

Bogdan took out his field glasses and focused on the rugged skyline, 'Looks pretty rough terrain, boss,' he lowered the binoculars, 'just like Afghanistan.'

Jack laughed, 'But not as cold, eh, buddy?'

'Da, Afghanistan is one shit place.'

Six minutes later the Cessna increased altitude as it flew over the tallest mountain, then dropped down the south side and turned west towards the lower peaks. Bogdan was scanning the terrain when Jack pointed, 'Over there, big man. Three o-clock.'

The Russian fiddled with the focus, 'Da, that's it, boss.'

Jack pulled back on the throttles, reduced altitude and banked towards the Ras Wasin stronghold.

'I thought it would be bigger,' said Bogdan, still peering through the binoculars.

'I guess it's built for security, not comfort.'

'Da, is definitely secure. No way could you attack from land.'

Jack took the Cessna down. The altimeter read two thousand one hundred feet, the same altitude as the palace, 'The cable car looks to be the only access up the mountain. No roads or paths. Right, big man, get some pictures.'

The Russian took out his smartphone and began snapping away, as Jack made a second pass over the mountain top fortress.

'Not too many guards, boss, but there's a small ground-to-air missile system. Bogdan saw the flash before Jack, 'Oh, fuck, incoming, incoming.'

'Shit,' Jack pulled back on the column and rammed the throttles to full power. The twin engines roared as the aircraft, nose skyward, climbed towards the glaring sun.

Bogdan watched as the small missile streaked towards them, 'Starboard side. Starboard side. Almost on our ass.'

The engines screamed as Jack forced every ounce of power from them, 'Flare gun.'

'What?'

'In the foot well, the yellow box, Very Pistol. Get it out.'

Bogan leaned forward, straining against the gravitational pull as the Cessna continued to climb skyward. He flipped down the lid, removed the snub nosed pistol and one of the short fat flares, snapped the breach and just had time to insert it, before Jack put the plane into a gut wrenching nose dive, 'Where the fuck is it?'

Bogdan looked around and saw the missile change course, the rocket's vapour leaving a pure white trail in its wake. He slid open the side window and felt the hot air rush into the cabin.

'You ready?' shouted Jack.

'Da, say when.'

The plane lurched, as Jack, feet on both rudder pedals, banked hard to starboard, 'NOW.'

Bogdan fired, and then watched as the flare zoomed away in a crimson arc. Jack heaved back on the column, the engines roaring as the tiny aircraft pulled out of the nose dive; then shook violently, as the missile exploded twenty yards away.

Chapter Thirty Seven
'In On Our Arse'

Jack fought with the controls as the shock wave from the explosion thumped into the Cessna. He felt the impact from the shrapnel, as several warning light on the control panel lit up. Acrid black smoke streamed from the starboard engine, but there looked to be no fire. He quickly shut off the fuel supply and watched as the propeller ground to a halt. The billowing smoke reduced to a thin trail of vapour. He worked the rudder pedals and felt the positive response, then eased the column up slightly and grinned, 'We got rudder and aileron control.'

'But we only got one fucking engine, boss.'

Jack adjusted the throttle to the one remaining engine and corrected the trim. The plane lurched and was flying somewhat lob-sided, but he found it controllable, 'Yeah, but we still have another, big man.'

The Russian grinned, 'Da,'

Jack nodded to the rear seat, 'Is there any water in that cold box?'

Bogdan pushed off the lid and took out two small bottles, 'Water? I need fuckin vodka.'

Jack laughed, 'Yeah me too. I haven't had a drink for years, but I could do with one now.'

'We gonna be okay, boss?'

Jack turned and looked at his friend, 'Don't worry, we're gonna be fine. We've lost an engine, obviously. But we still have controls, which means we can fly and we can land. Eventually.'

'Eventually?'

'What I mean is, we've also lost a lot of fuel, so I doubt we're gonna make it back to Tripoli. We need to get as far north as possible, then put down somewhere safe. Once we're on the ground we'll worry about what happens next.'

Bogdan finished his water and pushed the empty bottle through the open window, then slid it shut, 'Great job back there, boss. You save our ass.'

'No. We saved our arse, buddy. Nice work with the flare gun.'

* * *

Tom had been back at the Corinthian for over two hours and heard nothing from the guys. The cell phones would be useless out over the desert, but they had the sat-phone, *So where the hell are they?*

He took out his smartphone and scrolled down the contacts, found the number, and was about to tap it when the phone beeped in his hand. The display read SAT-1. He quickly swiped the screen, 'Jack?'

'Hey, Tom.'

'Everything okay, mate?'

Tom heard Jack laugh, 'We're heading north in a two engine aircraft.'

'Okay?'

'But we only have one bloody engine.'

'For fuck sake, Jack what you been up to?'

'Tell you when we see you. We're not gonna make Tripoli. We're gonna have to put down in the desert.'

'Okay. You gonna dump fuel before you land?'

'We've about ten minutes of fuel left and I'll use that up. There's a road we should be able to set down on, so we're following that. Soon as we're on the ground I'll message you our position. Can you come get us?'

'Yeah, sure, I'll see if I can find a decent four-by-four and set off A-sap.'

'Great, cheers, buddy. Talk soon.'

'Good luck, Jack. Be safe.'

The altimeter read two hundred feet and the fuel warning light had just begun to flash. 'Okay time to put this bugger on the ground.'

'Thank fuck,' said Bogdan.

Jack eased the column forward and they began their slow decent, 'Tighten your seat belt, big man.'

The road below was sand covered, but Jack expected it to be tarmac beneath, 'Should be solid enough for us to put down on.'

'Let's fuckin hope so,'

Jack flipped the undercarriage lever and waited for the 'GEAR DOWN' light to come on.

'Shit. The landing gear isn't working, must have been hit when the missile exploded.'

The Russian reached for the manual handle, 'I crank it down,'

'No time. We're going in on our arse. Hold on.'

Chapter Thirty Eight
'Hang in There'

Tom took a cab to the Hertz car rental at the main airport. He looked over their small fleet of 4X4s' and found an almost new Mitsubishi Shogun, 'Let's have a look at this one, mate,' he said to the rentals clerk.

The young man fiddled in a bag of keys and found the Shogun's. He pressed the button and the lights flashed, as the doors unlocked. Tom climbed inside, found the bonnet release and pulled it. He checked the oil, water and brake fluid, and then closed the hood. The tyres and the two spares were examined and the clerk looked surprised to see him lie on the ground and check the suspension.

'Okay, I'll take this one. I'll need two extra fuel cans as well.'

After leaving the main airport, Tom drove to the short stay carpark and located Bogdan's old Land Rover. He found the three weapons and discreetly stowed them in the Shogun, He put one automatic under the driver's seat, one under the passenger seat and the shotgun was concealed in the back, along with all the ammunition. He left the parking area and quickly headed south, out of the city. Stopping at the first petrol station, he filled the two jerry-cans, bought two cases of water, three kilos of dates and a road map of Libya. Back in the vehicle he checked his watch, six-twenty. It'd be dark in an hour. He'd considered the dangers of desert driving at night, but leaving the guys out there, unprotected, for any longer than necessary was not an option. He switched on his satellite phone and checked the position Jack had sent earlier. He confirmed the location on the map and estimated a hundred and forty mile journey. *Just over three hours*, he thought, then tapped out a sat-phone message.

* * *

The crash landing had gone well; all things considered. Jack had cut the engine and hit the 'FUEL DUMP' seconds before the aircraft hit the road. He'd managed to keep the nose up and the first impact was taken by the belly of the fuselage, sending the stricken aircraft bouncing along the road like a flat stone across a smooth lake. Out of control, the plane skidded and spun violently off the road and down the small embankment, coming to a heart wrenching thud in a huge cloud of sand and dust.

'You alive, big man?'

'Niet,' said the Russian, as he burst out laughing.

Jack joined in the laughter as the cabin filled with dust. He coughed and spluttered as the cloying atmosphere filled his throat, 'That went well.'

Bogdan kicked open the jammed door and tumbled out onto the warm desert sand, 'Da, is best plane crash I have for years.'

Jack's door wouldn't open, so he clambered across the cabin and was helped out by the big Russian, 'You okay, boss?'

'My fuckin' back.'

'Okay, take it easy,' said Bogdan. He put Jack's arm over his shoulder and the two stumbled away from the twisted dust-covered wreck of the Cessna. He carefully set his friend down on the embankment, then went back to retrieve the cold box.

'Here, boss,' said the Russian, as he handed Jack a bottle of water.

Jack coughed several times and spat the dust from his mouth. He opened the bottle and swallowed half the contents, 'Cheers, buddy.'

They looked at each other, faces covered in dust, and the laughter returned.

'We're getting too old for this shit,' said Jack, as he finished the water. He coughed again, just as the sat-phone beeped. The message from Tom read, *ON MY WAY, HANG IN THERE.*

174

Chapter Thirty Nine
'Nine Lives'

Tom had been driving for over two hours, when the three lane highway south, turned into a smaller although still well maintained minor road. The full moon behind the broken cloud provided good visibility through the endless blackness that surrounded him. He had pushed hard down the motorway, but now his speed was cut by almost fifty percent on the sand covered 'B' road. He slowed the Shogun, pulled over and stopped on the roadside, then got out and walked to the rear of the truck, opened the back and took out a bottle of water. As he drank the warm liquid he looked at his watch. *Maybe an hour or so to go*, he thought, then switched on the sat-phone to check his location. He cross referenced his position on the road map and smiled. *Yeah, an hour should do it.*

He closed the back door as the moon slipped behind a bank of cloud. A sudden noise in the darkness alerted him. He quickly opened the back again and found the shotgun. He knelt behind the truck and raised the weapon to his shoulder, ready for whatever came out of the blackness. He waited for several seconds, his eyes straining, his ears desperate to pick up the sound again. Then there it was, getting closer. He could hear it clearly now, moving slowly towards him. His heart was pounding, the shotgun ready. Then, as the moon re-appeared, he stood up and smiled, as the family of feral camels trotted across the road.

'Go on,' he shouted, and then clapped his hands at the group of lumbering animals. He watched as they disappeared into the darkness and grinned. *Get a grip mate*, he thought.

The further south he travelled the worse the condition of the road became and although it didn't slow him down, it did make it less comfortable and more hazardous. He'd driven for a further seventy five minutes, when the sat-phone began to blink, indicating he'd arrived at the location. Slowing to five miles an hour he continued forward, flashing the headlights and sounding the horn, then grinned as the tip of the Cessna's wing appeared fifty yards in front of him. His grin widened when he saw the two dust covered figures appear at the side of the road.

The reunion was one of relief and humour, as the two survivors embraced Tom.

'Good to see you, buddy,' said Jack.

'Da, good to see you,' grinned the big Russian.

'Are you guys okay? Any injuries?'

'We're fine, Tom. Could've been a lot worse.'

'What the fuck happened?'

'Tell you all about it on the way back. Shall we go?'

'Let me top up the fuel, then we can haul ass. There's water and dates in the back if you need them.'

Fifteen minutes later the Shogun was heading north with Bogdan at the wheel. Jack, in the back seat, spent the next half hour bringing Tom up-to-date with their flight down, the discovery of the Ras Wasin stronghold and the subsequent encounter with the missile, resulting in the crash-landing on the road.

'Nine lives. You've definitely got nine fucking lives, Jack Castle.'

'I'm using 'em a bit too quickly, these days.'

Tom nodded, 'You've had plenty of time to work out the next move. What's the plan?'

Jack grinned, 'There're two ways to get into that place, the cable car or by helicopter.'

'Okay,' said Tom, 'and which one will we use?'

'Chopper, of course.'

'And they're just gonna let us fly in and land are they?'

'They are indeed,' Jack winked, 'our friend Colonel Gadhafi is gonna see to that.'

On the return journey, Tom reported on his morning with Marcel Dubois and the tour of *Golden Cloud 3*. The radioactivity on board needed to be investigated immediately and the Frenchman would be key in the search of the ship's engine room.

Jack looked worried, 'So *GC2* set sail over thirty six hours ago?'

'Correct, and the Frog said it has a range of four thousand five hundred miles. Which means it could reach the east coast of America,'

Jack looked at Tom for several seconds, 'So you think it's on its way to the Big Apple?'

'Shahadi has sworn to set off one of the bombs in New York, so it's fair to assume the first device is on-board and heading there.'

'Okay, I'll pass the word to London. They'll let the Yanks know.'

Tom nodded, 'Good. We need to get on board *GC3* again. I'll contact Dubois soon as we get back to Tripoli.'

'Yeah,' said Jack, 'and tell him there's no fucking about, we all need to get on board.'

Bogdan turned to Jack, 'So what about Ras Wasin and Mr. Shahadi, boss?'

'We get on board Dubois's ship first and secure the bomb. Then we go after that bastard.'

It was after three in the morning by the time they arrived at the Corinthian. In the foyer Jack stretched the muscles in his back, 'Let's get some sleep. Meet for breakfast at o-seven-hundred and we'll go over everything again.'

'Yeah, okay,' said Tom. 'I'll call Dubois now and tell him to meet us at the dock entrance.'

Jack nodded, 'Right, I'm gonna call London, let them know about *Golden Cloud 2*. They can get the American navy to intercept.'

'Shit,' said Tom.

'What is it?

'Missed calls from Dubois, while I've been out in the dessert.'

Bogdan and Jack watched as Tom repeatedly tried to call the Frenchman, 'No reply.'

'It's the middle of the night. He'll be asleep,' said Jack.

'No, if he's been trying to contact me, something's wrong. Hold on I have voice-mail.' Tom tapped the screen and the engineer's voice was heard on the speaker, '*Golden Cloud 3 leaving now.*'

'Fuck,' said Jack, 'what time was the message.'

Tom looked at the screen, 'Eight-thirty. They set sail over seven hours ago.'

Chapter Forty
'The Souk'

Jack hadn't slept again, and was down in the restaurant just after six-o-clock. He was on his third cup of tea when Tom walked in, 'Morning.'

'Morning, Tom. You get any sleep, buddy?'

'Not much.'

The waiter arrived and they ordered more tea and coffee, just as Bogdan entered the dining room. The big Russian came back from the breakfast buffet with a heavily laden plate and two large glasses of juice.

'Hungry, big man?' said Jack.

Bogdan grinned, 'Da, yesterday's flight catering was pretty poor.'

'And their planes don't seem to get where they're supposed to either,' said Tom.

They all laughed when Jack said, 'But they do a mean crash landing.'

Breakfast over, they moved into the big bar lounge and took a table away in the corner.

'I spoke with London last night. They'll have probably been in contact with the Yanks by now. Their navy should have no problem locating and intercepting *GC2*.'

Tom nodded, 'What about Dubois's ship?'

'I informed London the third yacht had sailed. The Brits have a couple of destroyers in the Med, they could use them to intercept, but as the second target is allegedly Tel Aviv, I think they'd get onto the Israelis and leave it to them.'

'Just leaves Ras Wasin,' said Bogdan, 'put a fuckin cruise missile into it?'

Jack and Tom grinned, 'If only we could,' said Jack, 'but Libya's a sovereign nation, we can't just initiate an airstrike on one of Gadhafi's palaces.'

Tom rubbed his hands together in mock delight, 'So we're going after Shahadi?'

'Yep, and this is how we're gonna do it,' Jack took out a piece of paper and handed it to Bogdan, 'Think you can get us these items, big man?'

The Russian read down the list and grinned, 'We going to fancy dress party, boss?'

'Something like that, yeah.'

Bogdan passed the list to Tom, who looked at Jack, 'This is gonna get us into Ras Wasin?'

'Yeah. Well, that and one of Gadhafi's helicopters.'

A few minutes after nine, Bogdan left the Corinthian. He took a taxi out to the airport and recovered his Land Rover, then headed back into the city. He was unsure where to get hold of the items on Jack's list, but then remembered the souk in the 'old town'. He drove down to the port area and parked in a side street, a block away from the old market.

The souk was packed with locals, interspersed with the occasional tourist, the noise was deafening, as hawkers, traders and customers all chattered at once. Bogdan did not enjoy the oppressive heat in the enclosed narrow alleyways, nor the smell of sweat, spices and cigarette smoke that permeated the still air. He pushed his way through the complaining crowd and finally found a shop selling the kind of items Jack needed.

The driver parked the little Fiat around the corner from Bogdan's vehicle and quickly followed the Russian into the busy souk. It was easy enough to keep the big man insight as he stood head and shoulders above the jostling crowd. The Fiat driver saw him enter a shop and took a seat in the small café opposite, then watched bemused, as the Russian haggled with the persistent storekeeper. Taking out his smartphone, he discreetly took several pictures of the two men, then quickly tapped out a text. After attaching the photos he pressed SEND.

Chapter Forty One
'Fancy Dress'

It was mid-afternoon when Bogdan returned from his shopping expedition. Tom was already in Jack's room when the Russian entered, 'You get everything, big man?' said Jack.

'Da, couple of things a problem, but I find.'

Tom grinned, 'Let's have a look then?'

The Russian carefully emptied the contents of several bags onto the bed. Proudly displaying his purchases, he said, 'This was the most problem to find. Is okay, boss?'

Tom began laughing as Jack took the item and carefully fitted it onto his head, 'Sorry, mate. But you look a right dick with that on.'

Jack caught a glimpse of himself in the mirror, 'Don't I just. Okay, gentlemen, let's see how everything fits.'

The next fifteen minutes was filled with ribald comments, disparaging jibes and laughter, until everyone was ready. As Jack put on the big sunglasses the laughter stopped and Tom said, 'Bloody hell, this might just work.'

Bogdan was dressed in a rather tight fitting black business suit, white shirt and black tie. A peaked cap and sunglasses completed the outfit. Tom stood next to him in a slightly oversized military uniform, complete with polished belt, insignia and medals. The ornate cap and sunglasses gave him the look of a senior military officer. But it was Jack's outfit that brought the laughter to an end. He wore a long dark brown dish-dash, with a matching heavy silk shawl wrapped around his shoulders, a brown skull cap, topped a thick black curly wig and a pair of overly large sunglasses obscured most of his face. To anyone but his closest staff, he was the image of the ruler of Libya, Colonel Muammar Gaddafi.

An hour later they were at their usual corner table in the bar lounge, beers and coke in front of them. Tom raised his glass and said quietly, 'Here's to the three stooges. If we don't get shot, or we don't capture Shahadi, we can always put on a cabaret act in that gear.'

Jack looked around the room and then leaned forward, 'So, tomorrow we get a limo from the car hire at the airport, then find somewhere discreet to get into our fancy dress. Bogan, our trusty chauffeur and minder, will drive us to the dock yard. Tom will snarl at the security guards, who will shit themselves when they see the president has shown up unannounced. I'll be in the back looking like one bad-ass dictator. We commandeer one of the naval helicopters and take off for a little flight down to see our buddy, Mr Shahadi, at Ras Warin. All seems pretty easy to me, guys.'

The Russian finished his beer, 'I fuckin hope so, boss.'

Jack grinned, 'What could possibly go wrong?'

Tom leaned forward this time, 'We could be caught impersonating the dictator and shot. We could get arrested at the security gate, and shot. We could get caught by the Libyan navy, and shot. In fact tomorrow we are gonna have to work very hard to not actually get shot. And, if we do manage to get down to Ras Wasin, we could end up with a rocket up our arse.'

'Yeah, but apart from that,' smiled Jack, 'we should be okay.'

In the foyer, a tall dark haired man stood reading a local paper. From his position next to the concierge's desk, he could see across to the far corner of the bar, where the three men were huddled. He looked at his watch and then folded the paper, put it under his arm and left the hotel. It had been a long hot day following the Russian and he could smell the stale sweat on his shirt. Now all he wanted was a cool shower. The information he had bribed out of the souk vendors was interesting. It was clear these three intended to impersonate someone, but whom? It seemed a strange plan, but then again these guys were British.

He walked down the drive and out through the main gates. The Fiat 500 was parked a short way along the approach road. As he pressed the fob button the lights blinked and the locks clicked open. Once inside he quickly tapped out and sent two short text messages. He smiled as he starting the engine and then pulled out into the stream of traffic.

Chapter Forty Two
'Washington, London, Tel Aviv'

In the Cabinet Room Colonel Avi Rishom was seated with a dozen other high-ranking Israeli officers and ministers. Several heated conversations were occurring simultaneously, until the door opened and the Prime Minister entered. The men and woman around the table stood as he took his seat, 'Thank you everyone for coming at short notice. As you will have read from the brief before you, we have a tangible threat to our nation. I am sure we are all in agreement as to the only course of action.'

His Chief of Staff stood and cleared his throat, 'Sir, as you know we believe the vessel allegedly carrying the device is on its way to Tel Aviv. As you also know it will be in international waters when we intercept. All we need from you, Prime Minister, is the command to proceed with the mission.'

'Do I have an agreement from all here, that we have no issue with the apprehension of this ship in international waters?'

Everyone around the table nodded sombrely.

'Very well, General, you have a green light. You are authorised to use any and all means to ensure no harm comes to our nation.'

* * *

In the Oval Office the President stood at the window, arms folded, head back looking up at the clouds moving across the darkening sky. He turned, walked around the desk and leaned against the edge, 'Do we know where this ship is?'

The Vice President eased himself out of the big comfy couch, 'Yes, Mr. President, we're following it on satellite. It's currently twelve hundred miles from the east coast.'

'And the plan to intercept?'

The Chief of the General Staff rose from his seat, 'Sir, the aircraft carrier *George W Bush* will be within range in the next two hours. It will then deploy two Seahawk helicopters with full marine contingent. Our boys will stop the vessel and board her. Once we have the ship, the weapon will be neutralised and the ship and crew taken to Guantanamo.'

'Very good Admiral, please keep me advised at all times. Thank you everyone, that will be all for now.'

* * *

The rain beat heavily on Mathew Sterling's umbrella as he quickly walked along the Embankment. The meeting with the Secretary of Defence had gone well and the intelligence provide by Jack had been golden. The seizure of the bombs was paramount, but the capture of

Shahadi would be the cherry on the top. The only thing worrying Mathew was the assault on Gadhafi's stronghold. But if Jack and his guys pulled it off and their escape went to plan, then the world's biggest arms dealer would be theirs to interrogate for as long as they wanted.

Chapter Forty Three
'Dust Storm'

The wind had risen overnight and a dust storm was blowing over the city. They were in the hired 4X4, on their way to the Hertz office, 'This guy is gonna wonder what we're up to,' said Tom, 'one day we want a four-by-four, the next a bloody limo.'

'Probably think we're wealthy tourists, buddy.'

'Limo is niet problem. Problem is dust, can't fly in this, boss.'

Jack looked over his shoulder, 'Yeah, your right, big man. Let's hope it eases off soon.'

Tom dropped his friends and the bags at the Airport Hotel, then drove over to the car hire office. There were two people at the desk and he waited as the young woman took care of their documentation. The office door opened and the man who'd served him a couple of days ago entered, 'Hello again, sir.'

'Ah, good morning.'

'Returning the Shogun?'

'Yes, and I'm looking for a limousine today, please.'

The man didn't look surprised, 'Err yes, sir. We have two, but they're stored in the city. I can have one brought to your hotel?'

'That will be perfect. Let's do the paper work now. I'm at the Airport Hotel. Please have the vehicle delivered there.'

'Certainly, sir.'

'How long will that be?'

'We'll need to valet and fuel it first, then drive it out here. Perhaps two hours?'

'That's fine. Can you get someone to drive me over to the hotel, please?'

'Let's finish the paperwork and I'll drive you over myself. Will you need a chauffeur with the limousine, sir?'

'No thank you. I have my own driver.'

Jack and Bogdan were waiting in the reception area when Tom returned, 'Gonna be a couple of hours before the limo gets here, guys.'

'That's okay, buddy. We sit it out here until the weather improves.'

'Da, is good we wait. Maybe in couple hours will be clear.'

Jack slapped the big Russian on the back, 'Let's get a drink.'

They picked up their holdalls and went into the busy bar area, 'Must be a lot of delayed flights,' said Tom, 'this place is packed.'

'Over here,' said Bogdan, as he pushed his way to a table being vacated.

'I'll get some drinks,' said Tom.

Once at the table Jack looked around the busy bar. No one seemed to be paying them any attention. He noticed the tall dark-haired guy at the end of the bar and for a second their eyes met. Jack thought he recognised him, but then the man looked away and continued reading his paper, 'You're happy with the range of the Hind, big man?'

Bogdan swallowed half his beer, 'Da. Hind is great Russian helicopter, easy travel four hundred miles.'

Tom leaned forward, 'It's a hundred and fifty to Ras Wasin, then another two hundred across the border to Hassi Messoud, so we should be fine.'

Jack raised his coke, 'If we can blag our way into the palace, get out and over the border to Algeria, we're home and dry.'

They all raised their glasses and clinked them together, 'Da, nastrovia.'

'Our old pal in Hassi Messoud is ok?' said Tom.

Jack smiled, 'Yeah, I spoke with Ahmed Benhour and he has no problem letting us land on his operations base.'

'So, if the fancy dress works, we could actually pull this off.'

'Da, and if not, we'll be dead anyway, so nothing to worry about.'

Squeezed into a corner at the far end of the bar, the tall dark-haired man appeared to read his paper. All around him, people jostled and shouted for service, but he never moved or took his eyes off the three men sitting twenty yards away.

Chapter Forty Four
'Boarding Parties'

Golden Cloud 2 was eleven hundred miles from New York when the big Seahawk helicopters arrived. As they circled above, the co-pilot in the lead chopper hailed the vessel, 'Sea-going yacht below, this is the United Sates Navy, please turn into the wind and stop your engines.'

'This is *Golden Cloud 2,* We are a privately owned vessel in international waters. You have no authority to stop us, sir.'

'*Golden Cloud,* we have reason to believe you are carrying suspect cargo. Turn into the wind and stop your engines immediately.'

The captain watched the clattering helicopters circle above, then, as the side doors above him slid open and the gunners appeared, he clicked the mic, 'US Navy, this is *Golden Cloud.* Stand-by we are heaving-too.'

The swell was considerable, but with engines ticking over, the helmsman held the yacht steady. On deck, the captain watched as the first Seahawk took position directly over the stern. Within seconds four thick ropes dropped from the chopper, and, as the door gunner covered them, four marines slid down the ropes to the polished deck of *Golden Cloud.* The helicopter adjusted its position, and another four marines slid down onto the ship.

*　*　*

In the Eastern Mediterranean the Israeli naval cutter, *Eilat*, was holding position one hundred yards from *Golden Cloud 3*. An hour earlier, the heavily armed boarding party had taken control of the ship and secured the crew, while the six specialists, each wearing radiation protection and carrying a Geiger-counter undertook a thorough search of the vessel.

The Israeli officer had initially met with anger and indignation from the captain of *Golden Cloud*, but after being told his ship was suspected of transporting a nuclear device, had swiftly co-operated, while continually denying any knowledge of the heinous cargo.

Through the officer's earpiece came, 'Major Shapiro, sir?'

The major moved away from the ship's captain, 'Shapiro. Go ahead.'

'We have a high yield reading in the engine room, sir.'

'Very well. Have you found the device?'

'Not yet sir.'

'Move all the search team into the engine room. I want that place torn apart.'

195

Chapter Forty Five
'Ready Your Excellency?'

By one thirty the wind had dropped and the dust storm was clearing. The crowds in the bar and lounge of the Airport Hotel had begun to thin out as delayed passengers returned to the terminal. Bogdan had been outside to check on the weather, as he sat down he said, 'Looks better now. Maybe one hour, okay to fly.'

Jack nodded as Bogdan took his seat, 'Good, let's make a move now. Get into fancy dress somewhere and then down to the naval yard.'

Tom grinned, 'Showtime.'

The limousine had been delivered over an hour before and was parked in the VIP area close to the hotel entrance. Bogdan climbed into the driver's seat with Tom alongside. Jack took his place in the back, and became the subject of his friend's ribald and disparaging comments, all of which caused a lot of laughter in the big vehicle.

'You okay to drive this thing, big man?' said Tom.

'Da, is easy. I have big truck in Moscow.'

From the back, Jack piped up, 'Yeah, but it's not as long as this bloody thing.'

They eased away from the parking area and drove out onto the main road towards the city. Jack looked through the holdalls and found the weapons. He checked the two automatics and the shotgun were all fully loaded, then laid them carefully on the floor of the car.

'This should be okay,' said the Russian, as he turned off the main highway and drove up a tree lined side road. A further two hundred yards along the road there was a secondary track, just wide enough for the limo to get down. Bogdan turned off and eased the big vehicle twenty yards down the lane, then looked behind, 'This okay? Can't be seen from road.'

'It's good,' said Jack, as he too looked behind, 'let the dust settle before we get out.'

Several minutes later, the three men were in costume, but this time there was no laughter. They each knew the plan was extremely dangerous and failure would cost them dearly. Once dressed, Bogdan and Tom took an automatic each and concealed them inside their jackets. Jack had attached a short length of cord to the shotgun handle, which he looped over his shoulder and secreted under his robe.

Tom smiled, 'Ready to go, Your Excellency?'

Jack waved his hand regally, 'Yes, general. Please proceed.'

It was a few minutes before three-thirty when the limousine pulled up to the main gate of the naval dock yard. The two guards in the security shack ran out as the long black car slowed to a halt. Tom got out and in his best Arabic, arrogantly shouted at the men for not having the gates open. Jack lowered the window just enough for the guards to see him and almost smiled when he saw their reaction. One guard stood to attention and snapped a smart salute, as the other rushed back into the security shack to open the electronic gates. As Bogdan eased the big car through the entrance, the second guard scurried out and joined his colleague in the salute.

Tom had seen the naval heliport the day Marcel Dubois had escorted him into the dock yard. 'Stay on this road till you get to the big warehouse, then turn off and away from the harbour,'

The big Russian drove a little over the fifteen kilometre speed limit, people cars and trucks all moving to the side of the road as the long black car slid past.

Tom pointed ahead, 'Turn left after this building, stop in front of flight control'

Bogdan took the corner and the flight line appeared in front of them. There were several helicopters parked on the hardstand, from small two seaters bubble choppers, to large twin rotor Chinook troop carriers. At the far end of the stand were four Russian made Hind helicopter gunships. Two were fully laden with rockets, the other two without.

'Here.' said Tom.

Bogdan slowed down and came to a stop in front of a two story building, with a small control tower above it. As Tom got out, a young lieutenant arrived, snapped to attention and saluted. Tom casually returned the salute, and again in his best and most arrogant Arabic, said, 'Who is the senior office here today?'

'I am sir, Lieutenant Amid, sir.'

Tom sensed the officer was staring at his uniform and snarled, 'Stand to attention when I'm addressing you.'

The fearful young man stood rigid, head up, eyes forward.

'Sir. Yes, sir.'

'We will need a Hind immediately. Are they fully fuelled and ready to fly?'

'Sir?'

'I said, we need a helicopter immediately.'

The officer was about to speak, when Jack got out of the car. The man turned slowly, an amazed and confused look on his face when he saw the President standing in front of him.

'Lieutenant Amid,' snapped Tom, 'have you a Hind airworthy and ready to fly?'

'Sir. Yes, sir. I will have the pilots called straight away.'

'There will be no need. I shall fly his excellency today.'

Amid could feel the sweat running down his spine, he thought he was going to vomit, 'Sir. As you command. All Hinds are fuelled and airworthy.'

'Very good lieutenant. We will return in approximately two hours. You are not to inform anyone of our departure. Do you understand?'

'Sir. Yes, sir.'

'Not even your superior officer. No one must know.'

'Sir. Yes I understand.'

Jack climbed back into the car as Tom closed the door.

'Thank you, lieutenant. You're dismissed.'

The young officer saluted again and took one step back, as Tom climbed into the front seat. As the car drove away, Amid took a handkerchief from his pocket and wiped his face, then watched the sleek vehicle drive out to the flight-line, stopping several yards from the nearest Hind. He saw the officer get out and the chauffeur rush to open the doors of the helicopter. The big man dropped the steps, as the officer held open the limo door. The President left the vehicle and quickly walked to the aircraft, closely followed by the arrogant officer. The big chauffeur boarded last, pulled up the steps and secured the main hatch. Lieutenant Amid ran back into the building and up to the control tower. The two men at the flight control looked at him and waited for instruction, 'Give Hind-701 immediate clearance.'

'Yes, sir,' said the controller, 'Hind-701, you are clear for immediate take-off.'

Bogdan was quickly going through the pre-flight checks. Tom, in the co-pilots seat put on the head-phones, 'Thank you, Tower. 701 out.'

Chapter Forty Six
'Showtime'

After lifting off, Bogdan climbed to fifty feet and hovered for several seconds to get a feel for the controls, then said, to no-one in particular, 'Okay, da. Controls good. Systems good.' He expertly spun the aircraft one hundred and eighty degrees and gave a thumbs-up, 'Okay, we go.'

'Rock-n-roll, big man,' said Tom, a huge grin on his face.

The Russian increased rotor speed and the big ugly gunship climbed effortlessly into the warm afternoon sky.

They flew south west across the city, then out over the desert, Bogdan always listening to the chatter on the short wave, 'No talk of us on radio.'

'So far, so good,' said Tom, 'let's not count our chickens just yet though.'

Jack had taken off his Gadhafi costume and was standing behind the pilot's seat, 'Well done, big man. Great job.'

Tom turned to Jack, 'Let's just hope we can fool those fuckers at Ras Wasin as easily.'

Jack nodded and smiled, 'You were great, Tom. Real arrogant high ranking officer. Brilliant. You almost had me fooled.'

'Da, you were real bastard, boss. I think lieutenant crap his pants.'

They all laughed.

The late afternoon weather had cleared and the morning's sand storm had blown itself out. They'd picked up a tail wind from the north and the big helicopter clattered south-west over the endless miles of barren desert. Jack looked at his Rolex, 'What's our ETA, Bogdan?'

'Another forty miles, boss. About twenty minutes to location.'

'Okay, good. Let's go over the plan once more.'

Fifteen minutes later Bogdan shouted, 'Mountains ahead, boss.'

Jack was back into fancy dress, the shotgun concealed under the flowing robes. Tom and the Russian were in costume and after checking their weapons, secreted them inside their jackets. Bogdan slowly increased altitude and climbed gracefully above the range, then, in a flamboyant manoeuvre, dropped down the south side and banked the clattering aircraft towards the mountain top palace, 'Here we go again, boss.'

Tom picked up the mic, 'Ras Wasin, Ras Wasin. This is naval Hind-701. We require immediate clearance for landing.'

There was no response for several seconds, then the radio crackled, 'Hind-701, this is Ras Wasin control. We are not expecting any inbound aircraft. Please state your business?'

'Ras Wasin control. We are inbound with VIP's on board. Confirm clear to land . . .,' then Tom snarled into the mic, 'immediately.'

Several more seconds passed as the helicopter approached the stronghold, 'Naval Hind-701. Ras Wasin control. Yes, sir. You are clear to land. Windage is south east and fifteen knots.'

Tom grinned, 'Control. Inbound now. Stand by.'

Bogdan slowed forward speed to almost zero, as he eased the helicopter over the palace. The central courtyard doubled as a helipad, with landing lights, firefighting equipment and wind indicator pennants. A small executive helicopter was already parked off to the side, but there was still plenty of room to put the big Hind down safely.

'That's one of the *Golden Cloud* choppers,' said Tom.

'Da, maybe we should blow up before we go?'

'No need. I doubt, they'd have the balls to follow this thing. And if all goes well they won't suspect we're taking Shahadi against his will anyway.'

'Da, if all goes well.'

In the rear of the cabin, Jack watched Bogdan expertly manoeuvre the big helicopter into position over the landing area. The cumbersome aircraft shook as the rotor speed was reduced, gently descending onto the tarmac, in a cloud of swirling dust.

The dust settled and the big rotors slowed to a stop. At the edge of the helipad stood a line of security personnel, each dressed in para military uniform and armed with an AK47 assault rifle. They all wore baseball caps and sunglasses, the MIDCOM logo clearly visible on their breast pocket and cap. Jack smiled as he looked through the window, 'Shahadi's private army.'

'Yeah,' said Tom, 'let's hope we don't have to tangle with it.'

'And here's the man himself. Look,' Jack moved away from the window so Tom could see. A tall thin man had joined the security line up, 'So that's Shahadi?'

'That's him,' said Jack, a stern look on his face, 'Okay, guys. Showtime.'

Tom unlocked the main hatch and pulled the heavy door inwards, took hold of the guide rope and lowered the short set of steps to the ground. He quickly left the aircraft and stood to attention. As Jack emerged, Tom ostentatiously clicked his heels and snapped a very smart salute. Jack, in full Gadhafi-mode raised his left hand to the waiting parade, his right hand held a crisp white handkerchief over his mouth, covering his lower face.

The waiting guard of honour stood to attention, as Shahadi moved forward to greet the ruler of Libya. A few feet from Jack, Shahadi stopped and bowed slightly, 'Good afternoon, your Excellency. We are honoured to see you, sir.'

Jack nodded, raised his hand and mumbled through the handkerchief.

Tom stepped forward, 'His Excellency is suffering from severe laryngitis and has been ordered not to speak.'

The arms dealer looked puzzled, 'Ah, I understand.'

Tom continued, 'Can we get inside. The dusty atmosphere is not helping His Excellency.'

Shahadi stood to one side to allow the President to go ahead, but Jack mumbled again and waved his hand for him to proceed. The thin man scuttled forward and, as was hoped, led the way into the palace.

They followed the arms dealer up a thickly-carpeted staircase and into what appeared to be a large reception hall. The interior of the palace was elegantly furnished and in stark contrast to its Spartan exterior. At the far end of the hall were two large, highly polished doors, which Shahadi quickly opened. He stood back and bowed slightly as the President entered. As Jack walked into the room he nodded, and mumbled again through the white linen at his mouth.

'You have met Feisal before, Your Excellency.'

Jack nodded and waved to the man standing by the window.

Bogdan eyed up the big man, before closing the doors and quietly locking them.

Shahadi smiled his thin smile, 'May we get you some refreshments your, sir?'

Without answering, Jack dropped the handkerchief and deftly pulled the shotgun from his robes, as Bogdan and Tom drew their weapons.

The arms dealer took a few steps backwards, 'What the hell is this?'

Jack removed his sunglasses, 'You're fucked mate. That's what this is.'

Chapter Forty Seven
'Decoys'

It had rained all day. At Vauxhall Cross, Mathew Sterling was in his office and feeling good about the expected report from the Americans. He watched through the window, as the people, collars up, umbrellas turned against the rain, scurried along the Embankment.

He'd received the call that *Golden Cloud 2* had been located over eight hours ago. The choppers had to get to the ship and the boarding party would carry out the search, so news should be coming soon. Returning to his desk he pressed the intercom, 'Jennifer, could I have some tea, please?'

'Certainly, sir.'

He picked up a document and leaned back in the chair, just as the phone rang, 'Hello?'

'Excuse me, sir. The Director General would like you to meet her immediately, please.'

'Thank you, Jennifer. Forget the tea for the moment.'

'Yes, sir.'

Mathew stepped out of the lift and was greeted by Gareth, the DG's personal assistant, 'Good afternoon, sir.'

'Good afternoon.'

'You can go straight in. She's waiting for you.'

Sterling knocked on the door and heard the usual, 'Come.'

The Director General sat, with hands clasped, elbows resting on the fine leather top of her desk. As he entered, she stood and walked towards him, 'Mathew. Please have a seat.'

'What's the news, ma'am?'

There was no answer for several seconds, and then, 'Not good I'm afraid.'

'Ma'am?'

'I heard from the Americans a few minutes ago. There is nothing untoward on *Golden Cloud 2.'*

Sterling looked puzzled, 'But we were advised of high radiation, we . . .'

The DG raised a hand, 'Apparently, the reading was from a minute quantity of plutonium concealed in the engine room. The ships were decoys, Mathew.'

'Have we heard from the Israeli's, ma'am?'

'Over an hour ago. It's the same story. We've been had.'

'Shit . . . Oh sorry ma'am. Please excuse me.'

'Not at all. Shit is correct.'

He stood up, 'I'll get onto my men in Libya, let them know the situation immediately.'

'Where are we down there, Mathew?'

'My guys, are in the process of apprehending Shahadi as we speak, ma'am.'

'Well, that is fortuitous. Please keep me informed. I want to know the minute we have him secure.'

'Yes, ma'am. If you will excuse me.'

'Of course. Thank you, Mathew.'

Chapter Forty Eight
'Samurai'

Shahadi looked at the three intruders, then their weapons. None had silencers. 'If you shoot me you are going to have a dozen of my men in here in seconds. You will not get away.'

Jack stepped closer, the shotgun pointed directly at the arms dealer's torso, 'I could cut you in half with this, you bastard. But we don't plan to kill you. Not yet anyway.'

Tom waved his automatic, 'Sit the fuck down.'

The thin man moved to a large silk-covered couch and did as instructed. Bogdan moved to get a better view of the big man by the window, 'You. Get over here.'

Feisal moved slowly away from the window and passed in front of a black lacquered Japanese table. On the table and mounted in an ornate stand were two ancient Samurai swords. The speed in which he moved was exceptional for a man of his size. He had one of the swords in his hands before anyone realized. In a flash, he raised the gleaming blade above his head and charged at Tom, 'Ahhh . . .'

Jack turned and pointed the shotgun, but resisted the urge to shoot. Bogdan was already moving across the room, equally as fast as the bodyguard. Tom kicked a footstool at the charging Feisal, causing him to stumble to the floor, but the big man was on his feet and swung at Tom, who managed to side-step the deadly blade, but not enough. The razor edge sliced through his sleeve, opening a bloody gash in his upper arm. Tom fell back, the pain excruciating, as he raised his automatic to shoot the man towering over him.

'Nooooo . . .' yelled Bogdan.

Feisal spun to see the Russian coming at him, the other sword glinting above his head. He raised his weapon and slashed at the attacker, the clash of steel echoed around the vaulted room. The two men circled each other, then again the swords flashed, their speed making the blades almost invisible.

Jack kept the shotgun on the seated arms dealer, as he quickly moved over to help his wounded friend. He pulled Tom to his feet, as the fierce sword battle raged. Bogdan swung his sword from side to side, the long elegant blade scything through the air with a deadly whisper. Feisal parried and slashed again and again at the crazed Russian. As he retreated, he stumbled over the footstool, leaving an opening in his defence. Bogdan, in a move that could only be described as elegant, dropped to one knee and slashed horizontally.

Feisal's eyes widened as he dropped the sword and grabbed at his stomach. He stood for several seconds, mouth open, his lifeblood oozing through his fingers from the gaping wound in his abdomen. Bogdan stood and moved towards him, then watched as the bodyguard fell backwards onto the luxurious Persian carpet.

The room fell silent; the sound of Bogdan's heavy breathing was all that could be heard for several seconds. The big Russian was bent over; hands on knees, gasping for breath. The Samurai sword dripping blood onto the beautiful rug.

'Fuck me, big man. Where the hell did you learn to fight like that?' said Jack

Bogdan stood upright, his breathing steady. He wiped his mouth with the back of his hand,

'Never learned anywhere, boss. I'm just crazy bastard I guess.'

'Thank God, you're our crazy bastard,' said Tom, 'Cheers mate.'

The Russian grinned and threw the bloody sword behind the desk, 'Niet problem.'

Jack returned the grin, 'Bogdan, watch our host, please. Tom, keep pressure on the wound.'

Jack opened an antique cabinet at the side of the room and found it full of booze. He picked up a bottle of vodka and placed it on the desk, 'Over here, buddy.'

Tom winced, as Jack eased off his jacket, 'Bogdan. Knife?'

The Russian took a flick-knife from his pocket and tossed it to his friend. Jack clicked open the blade and cut away the blood soaked sleeve, then opened the vodka. 'Hold on, buddy.'

'Shit,' said Tom, as the liquid was poured over the wound.

Jack gave Tom the bloodied sleeve, 'Hold this against the wound,' then went to the desk. After opening several draws he found a stapler.

'Oh, you're shitting me?' said Tom.

'Take a slug of that vodka.'

Tom gulped down a large mouthful of the alcohol.

Jack held the flesh together, 'Ready?

Several minutes later Tom was back in uniform. Jack had closed up the wound and dressed it using the other sleeve from Tom's shirt. Although not perfect, it was a good field dressing that would hold till they got to the base in Algeria. 'Okay, keep an eye on our friend here, buddy. Bogdan and I'll check the place over for any intel.'

Jack and the Russian quickly went through the desk and cupboards in the big room, 'Laptop and some files,' said Bogdan.

Jack looked up from the drawers, 'Bag them up, mate. I've got three cell-phones and a satellite-phone. We should be able to get plenty of intel from these.'

'Whoa . . .' said Bogdan.

Tom looked across the room, 'What you got?'

The Russian placed an open briefcase on the desk.

Jack turned and flicked through the contents of the case, 'Fuck sake, big man. Could be four maybe five million dollars here.'

'Five million,' said Shahadi, 'take it and forget about me.'

Jack looked at the man, 'No amount of money will get you released,' then closing the lid he pushed the case towards Bogdan, 'but we will take it. Here you go big man, that's for you.'

'You sure, boss?'

Jack winked, 'You earned it, buddy.'

'I agree,' said Tom, 'Buy yourself a few of vodkas.'

The Russian's face lit up and the huge grin appeared, 'Spasibo bolshoi.'

'Right,' said Jack, 'show time again.'

They were back in costume, Jack in front, Shahadi with Tom, and Bogdan at the rear. After leaving the room, Bogdan quietly closed and locked the big doors, taking the key, he dropped it into a nearby Chinese vase. They moved quickly through the reception area, down the stairs and out to the courtyard. Several security men were waiting outside, and, as the group emerged, they all came smartly to attention. Jack, the white handkerchief to his face, raised a hand in salute and moved swiftly to the Hind.

Tom leaned in close to Shahadi, 'We want you alive, but say anything and you're a dead man.'

The arms dealer followed Jack and climbed into the aircraft, quickly followed by Tom. Bogdan pulled up the steps and secured the main door, then rushed to the flight deck. The Russian didn't bother with any pre-flight checks and within four minutes of boarding the rotors were spinning, kicking up a dust cloud that covered the on-looking security men.

The radio crackled, 'Hind-701, Ras Wasin control. You are clear for take-off, sir.'

In the chopper, no one bothered to reply.

Chapter Forty Nine
'Let me tell you a story'

The engines roared as Bogdan turned the throttle to ninety percent power. The rotors, almost invisible, bit into the air and lifted the big helicopter away from the mountain top palace.

Jack found a case of mineral water in the storage locker, along with a First Aid kit. He took a couple of bottles and a packet of painkillers and after securely tying Shahadi into his seat, went up to the flight deck. He looked back from the pilot's window and watched Ras Wasin slip away behind them, 'Great job, big man,' he said to the Russian. Then turning to Tom, 'How's the arm, buddy? Here's some water and pain killers.'

'It's okay. Nothing to worry about.'

We'll get it treated and dressed properly, once we get to Ahmed Benour's base.'

'How's our guest?' said Tom.

'All tucked up and tied into his seat. I'm gonna go have a chat with him shortly.'

Tom grinned, 'We did it, mate. We fucking did it.'

'Yeah, thanks to you, Bogdan.' he handed the Russian a bottle of water, 'That was some sword fight.'

They all laughed.

Jack patted the Russian on the shoulder, 'What's our ETA at Hassi Messoud, big man?'

'Punching co-ordinates into navigation computer now, boss.'

Jack looked out at the setting sun, 'Gonna be dark when we get there.'

'Da. Okay, we got one hundred eighty five miles to go. Arrive Hassi Messoud, about one hour forty.'

'Excellent, I'll contact Ahmed Benour on the sat-phone. Let him know to expect us.'

'Good idea,' said Tom, grinning, 'otherwise they're gonna shit when they see a Russian gunship landing on their base.'

They all laughed again.

Jack sat across from the arms dealer and after gulping down half a bottle of water, said, 'You wanna drink?'

Shahadi slowly moved his head from side to side, 'Who are you? Who are you working for? CIA?'

'Don't worry about us, mate. You should be worried about yourself. Your arse is well and truly in the wringer.'

The arms dealer smiled his thin smile and narrowed his eyes, 'You think so?'

'I fucking know so, you bastard. You're gonna pay for what you did to Farida. Never mind your grand enterprise with the plutonium.'

'Let me tell you a little story, my friend. My father was Indian, a sergeant in the British army during the war. He was wounded quite badly in Malaya and returned to Kerala, where he met and married my mother. He was a drunk and a brute and beat her regularly. When I was fourteen I found her dead. He had beaten her to death. He disappeared for a few days and returning after she was buried, made up some story about an intruder, but it was he who killed her.'

'I'm not really interested in your life story, mate.'

'Please. Indulge me,' smiled the arms dealer, 'not long after that he began going to my sister's room at night. She was twelve years old. I could hear her whimpering as I lay in my bed, I was afraid, but glad at the same time. I was happy he did not come into my room. But I was disgusted with myself for not helping my young sister. One day I came home from school and she too was dead. She'd taken rat poison; would probably have died in agony.

That night, as my father lay drunk in his bed, I went to his study and took his army revolver. I crept into his room and stood over him for many minutes, watching that animal lying there, his mouth open, grunting, snoring, the vile smell of alcohol and sweat filled my nostrils. I cocked the revolver and slowly put the barrel into his open mouth. His eyes opened and I looked right into them . . . as I pulled the trigger.'

Jack looked at the man opposite, 'Like I said, I'm not really interested.'

Shahadi smiled the thin smile again, 'Please. Let me finish. There's a moral to the tale, as it were.'

'Whatever.'

'That night I left the house with the revolver and several other guns he'd collected. I took what little money we had and made my way to Bombay where I sold the weapons. I ended up in Beirut, selling weapons to the various militia and I've been doing it ever since. So you see, Mr. whoever you are. I always do what I have to, to survive, and I shall certainly survive this situation, of that you can be sure.'

Jack grinned, 'Like I said. Whatever.'

After checking his Rolex, Jack went to his hold-all and took out the satellite-phone, switched it on and waited several seconds for the signal. He looked at the screen and then moved to the rear of the aircraft, away from the arms dealer. Four missed calls from London.

'Mathew?'

'Jack. Hello. You okay? We've been trying to contact you.'

'Yeah, we're fine. We've been a little busy.'

'Where are you?'

'In Algerian airspace. On route to Haasi Messoud.'

'And Shahadi?'

'We've got him.'

'Thank God. Some good news at least.'

'What d'you mean? Good news.'

'The ships, Jack. There are no bombs on the ships. They were decoys.'

Chapter Fifty
'Benour'

Once across the border, Bogdan descended to eighty feet and flew as low as the terrain would allow, thus avoiding Algerian radar. In the distance he could now see the lights of the city sparkling like a pool of iridescent algae on the surface of the black dessert.

Hassi Messoud, in North Eastern Algeria, had grown from a remote town into a small city, thanks to the discovery of oil in the 1950's. The Algerian State Oil Company; always referred to as, ALSOCO, had a large operations base on the outskirts of the city. The base had its own heliport, used on a daily basis for transporting workers to and from the surrounding oilfields.

As the aircraft neared the base, Tom picked up the mic, 'ALSOCO control, this is Hind-701, do you read me?'

The radio crackled, 'Hind-701, this is control, we read you loud and clear. We are expecting your arrival and have eyes on you. Landing lights are deployed and you are clear to land from the west.'

Tom turned and smiled at Bogdan, 'Thank you, control, Hind-701 inbound.'

The big helicopter shuddered as the power was reduced and the aircraft slowly descended to the helipad. As the dust settled, the huge rotors came to a stop, 'We made it, boss,' said a smiling Bogdan.

Tom returned the smile, 'Yeah, we did, well done, mate. Well done.'

Jack, now devoid of the Gadhafi fancy dress, opened the main door and lowered the steps.

Shahadi was untied from his seat and unceremoniously pulled to the exit. Tom and Bogdan arrived from the fight deck. Tom smiled and gestured towards the door, 'After you, Your Excellency.'

All except Shahadi, laughed.

At the edge of the landing area stood a small group of men, the tallest, Jack immediately recognised as his old friend Ahmed.

In his earlier life, Ahmed Benour was a trooper in the French Foreign Legion. He'd served as a mercenary in the Belgian Congo, as well as several other unpleasant wars on the African continent. He was now the Chief Security Officer for ALSOCO. At almost sixty years old he was still an imposing figure. Standing over six feet tall, broad shouldered and athletic, he was physically capable as well extraordinarily intelligent, the two key assets of a good soldier and security officer.

Jack had met Ahmed in South Africa when they both worked security for a gold mining company. There was an explosion underground and a dozen local workers were trapped. The local emergency team were reluctant to effect a rescue due to the nature of the explosion and were happy to accept their fellow countrymen were dead or dying. It was Ahmed Benour who'd physically thrown the emergency team off the site and volunteered to go below ground. Jack Castle was the only other man who stepped forward that day and together they saved the lives of eight of the twelve trapped men. They had remained friends ever since.

With his right hand over his heart Benour smiled, 'Salaam Alaikum, my old friend. It is good to see you.'

'Alaikum Salaam, sidi.'

They shook hands and embraced, then Jack introduced Tom and Bogdan, after which Benour said, 'And this is our special guest?'

Jack turned and looked at Shahadi, 'Can you accommodate him somewhere secure?'

The Arab waved his hand and the three men at the edge of the helipad came forward, 'Put him in our storage shack. Twenty four hour guard. And get him some food and drink. No one speaks to him.'

As Shahadi was led away he turned to Jack, the thin smile ever present, 'Whatever I have to do, to survive. Remember that.'

'We'll see,' said Jack.

Ahmed looked at his friend, 'Come. I have accommodation for you all. We will eat soon and you can tell me what all this is about.'

An hour later the four men were in Benour's villa and after an excellent lamb tagine sat around in the comfortable lounge, Bogdan and Tom enjoying a welcome cold beer, Ahmed and Jack drank thick Turkish coffee and picked at a large tray of baklava.

'So, this man knows where the bombs really are?' said Benour.

Jack put down his cup, 'Yes. The ships, as I said, fooled everyone. But he will tell us where the bombs are.'

'The problem you have my friend is, when are they due to go off? You do not have time for Western niceties. I can have the information extracted for you?'

'Da, I can help,' grinned Bogdan.

Tom smiled and took another gulp of beer, 'We're supposed to be civilised, gentlemen.'

Jack got up and went to the large patio windows; the full moon was reflected in the small swimming pool, the lights around the edge attracting tiny fireflies. 'We spoke at length on the chopper. He knows he has a great bargaining chip. He'll tell us where the bombs are, only if he is cut a deal.'

Benour poured more coffee, 'So just lie to him. Promise him anything.'

'He's not an idiot. It'll take more than a promise. He's said he wants to talk only to the top people in London. He'll give us the location of the bombs, plus a lot more information on his terrorist clients. But only when we get him to London.'

'So you will do as he demands, my friend?'

'There's a plane coming to pick us up in the morning. We'll leave from the local airport with diplomatic documents. No one will know who we, or more importantly, who he, is.'

Benour stood up, 'So there's nothing to be done until morning.'

'Except drink more beer,' said Bogdan.

They all laughed.

Chapter Fifty One
'Homeward Bound'

Jack hadn't slept well. He'd succumbed to a disturbing nightmare that warranted a call to Nicole in the early hours of the morning. Although being wakened from a deep sleep, she was more than happy to hear his voice and calm his dreamtime fears. They'd talked for a long while, until he finally let her go just before five-thirty. Later, and after a prolonged shower he used the courtesy shaving kit to get rid of several days' stubble. He looked at his Rolex, and at seven o-clock walked over to Ahmed's villa.

Tom was already on the patio with the Arab. A substantial breakfast was laid out and as Jack approached Benour stood and shook hands, 'Salaam, my friend. How did you sleep?'

'Fine, thank you, Ahmed.'

'Come, eat something.'

Jack took a seat in the shade, 'You okay, Tom? How's the arm?'

Tom grinned and rubbed his bicep, 'A lot better with your bloody staples removed.'

The big Russian's shadow fell across the table as Bogdan arrived. In a deeper voice than usual and with a strained smile, he   greeted the three men, 'Good morning.'

Again Benour stood and shook hands, 'Come, my friend, there is plenty to eat.'

'Niet, niet, no food. Just coffee and water. Plenty water.'

The others laughed as the Arab said, 'I take it you enjoyed the beers, Mr. Bogdan.'

The Russian just groaned.

After breakfast, Benour stood up, 'What time is your plane expected?'

Jack looked at his watch, 'London said eleven o-clock. It'll do a fast turnaround and we'll be back at RAF Northolt this afternoon.'

'Home in time for tea,' said Tom.

'Yes indeed,' said Jack, 'Right, if everyone's finished, I think I'll go and see how our friend Mr. Shahadi is today?'

Benour drove the four men to the airport himself. He knew all the security and official staff and was welcomed by each uniformed person he met. The airport was not busy as far as commercial traffic was concerned, with only one international flight a day from Tunis. The majority of arrivals were from various oil company charters that came in from Europe. And the incidents of anyone being processed with 'diplomatic papers' was non-existent.

'Our documents will be on the plane,' said Jack, 'we'll need to wait out here for the courier to arrive.'

'We got another hour at least,' said Tom, 'let's get a drink in the bar,'

The bar area was busy, and extremely raucous with homeward-bound oilfield contractors, mostly American and French. The only seats available were outside and as the temperature was in the low forties, no one cared for an alfresco drink. Tom pushed to the counter and shouted the order to the overworked staff. With drinks in hand the five men left the area and found a quieter corner next to the main entrance.

Jack raised his glass, 'Cheers, Ahmed. Thank you for all your help.'

'No problem, my friends. I hope our next meeting will be in happier circumstances, inshallah.'

The four raised their glasses in a toast, only Shahadi stood silent, discreetly handcuffed to Bogdan.

An hour later, the Arrivals Board indicated flight UK-650 from London had landed.

'That's us,' said Jack.'

Fifteen minutes later, two very well dressed young men appeared in the Departures area.

'That's gotta be them,' said Tom with a grin, 'only diplomats would show up in business suits.'

Jack grinned then moved towards the men, 'Good morning.'

'Good morning, sir,' the accent was pure public school and Cambridge.

'You guys from London?'

'That's correct, sir.'

Jack flashed his genuine passport, 'You're here to get me and my team out.'

'Yes, sir. We have documentation to extract four. All diplomatic, so there won't be any problems.'

'Very good. I have a local contact with me who's well respected by the officials here. I'll ask him to stand by in case of any issues.'

'No need, sir. I can assure you the signatures on your documentation come from the highest authority.'

'Fair enough. Give me a moment please, gentlemen.' Jack returned to the group.

'Everything cool?' said Tom.

'We're good, these guys seem confident we should have no problem getting out.'

Benour shook hands with Tom and Bogdan, then turned to Jack, 'Goodbye, my old friend. Allah be with you.'

'And you, Ahmed. Thanks again for all your help.'

After they embraced Benour said, 'What do you want me to do with the Libyan helicopter?'

Jack winked, 'You keep it, buddy. I'm sure you'll find a buyer for it. Oh, and there's a couple of shooters in there as well. '

The big Arab grinned, then walked away.

Chapter Fifty Two
'Tariq & Nasir'

In New York's, Times Square, it was a few minutes
before noon Eastern Standard Time, when Tariq Rabbani
emerged from the packed subway and out onto the busy
street. His senses were assaulted by the lights from a
hundred digital signs, the noise of the busy midday
traffic and the bustling crowds. He stood amazed at the
spectacle, so many people, like ants, each one running,
pushing and shoving the other to live their lives. The day
was cool for late spring, but carrying the heavy back-
pack had made him sweat in the subway and he could
feel the perspiration trickle down his spine. He was
jostled by the people as they pushed by, so he moved to
the side of the pavement and gazed up at the huge bank
of animated signs towering above him. He never
believed he would ever come to this place, but now he
was here and soon he would be in paradise. In Tripoli,
Mr. Feisal had shown him how to arm the device. Now
his fingers found the button and he closed his eyes for
several seconds. He took a deep breath and quietly spoke
the words . . . 'Allah O Akbah.'

* * *

Seven hours ahead of New York, Nasir Yacoub sat in the food court of the huge Ramat Aviv Mall; he could have chosen any, but this was the biggest in Tel Aviv. He sipped an ice cold pineapple juice and watched as the condensation ran down the side of the glass onto the table in front of him. The mall was noisy with early evening shoppers, but his mind was clear, he was at peace. A mother and child walked past and he thought of his family in Syria. He smiled at the child and took another sip of his juice, the saccharine taste sweet on his palette. He placed the glass on the table and slipped a hand into his pocket, he remembered Feisal's instructions and now the weapon was armed. With head tilted back he looked up at the huge dome above him, then, with eyes closed he quietly spoke the words . . . 'Allah O Akbah.'

Chapter Fifty Three
'We're Home'

The flight from Algeria to RAF Northolt was comfortable and smooth. The service was friendly and the food good, with everyone except Shahadi enjoying a pleasant lunch. The banter between Bogdan, Jack, and Tom was ribald and good humoured, while the two diplomats sitting at the rear of the aircraft chatted quietly between themselves. Only the arms dealer remained silent.

A few minutes after three o-clock, the FASTEN SEAT BELTS signs blinked. Jack had fallen asleep an hour before. Tom shook him awake, 'Seat belt, buddy. We're home.'

The small jet came smoothly into land and, as it turned off the end of the runway, a small pickup truck pulled in front, an illuminated FOLLOW ME sign on the roof. The sleek aircraft followed the truck to the far side of the base and into a large hangar, empty except for two gleaming black Jaguars, a Range Rover, and an Air Police van. Next to the cars stood several men, some in RAF uniform the others in civilian clothes.

Jack was fully expecting his brother to be there and turned to Tom, 'I don't see Mathew?'

Tom grinned, 'He's a big shot now, mate. Not likely to see him fraternising with us mere mortals.'

Jack shook his head slightly, 'He said he'd be here.'

The two young diplomats moved to the front of the plane and after the door was opened and the steps dropped, quickly exited to the waiting group of men. As Jack and the others left the plane the group came forward. The senior air-force officer spoke first, 'Good afternoon, gentlemen. I'm Wing Commander, Simpson.'

Jack offered his hand, 'Good afternoon, sir. I'm Jack; this is Tom, and Bogdan.'

Simpson didn't seem to mind the fact that no surnames were used. 'Welcome to RAF Northolt, gentlemen. I have orders to secure an individual,' then looking at Shahadi, continued, 'and I take it this is the person in question?'

Jack stepped to one side, 'Yes, sir. He's all yours.'

'Sergeant.'

The air- police sergeant marched smartly forward, 'Sir.'

'Secure this man, sergeant. Maximum security.'

'Yes, sir.'

Two other police officers moved forward, one handcuffing himself to Shahadi, who was then marched away to the waiting van. As he walked away the arms dealer turned to Jack, the thin smile annoying as ever,

'Whatever I have to do, to survive. Remember that . . . Jack.'

One of the waiting civilians stepped up, 'Good afternoon, gentlemen. We're here to take you to Vauxhall Cross.'

Jack nodded, 'Okay, thank you. Hold on a second, please.' Jack quickly went over to the Range Rover as the two young diplomats were climbing in, 'Hey, thanks for your help, guys.'

The young men smiled, 'You're welcome, sir.'

As they walked to the waiting vehicles, Bogdan leaned close to Tom, 'What's Vauxhall Cross, boss?'

Tom smiled and winked, 'MI6.'

Jack climbed into the front seat and as the sleek car moved slowly away, snapped a casual salute to Wing Commander Simpson.

On leaving the base the Jaguars picked up a police escort, consisting of two motorcycle outriders. With the bikes out in front and the blue flashing lights on all vehicles, the ride from Northolt into the city only took a little over thirty minutes.

The cars crossed over the River Thames at Vauxhall Bridge, and turned sharp left towards the underground parking of Vauxhall Cross, the home of the British Secret Service. At the gate house, the driver flashed his ID and a few seconds later the heavy steel bollards across the entrance sank into the ground. The vehicles moved into the secure area and stopped in front of a set of lift doors. A tough looking security guard stood next to the entrance and nodded as two men from the rear Jaguar flashed more ID's. He ran a key-card through the mechanism and the elevator doors slid silently open. Tom, Bogdan, and Jack entered the lift, quickly followed by the two men. A few seconds later they entered a smart reception hall.

One of the escorts pointed to a waiting area. 'Please have a seat, gentlemen. Someone from upstairs is on their way down.'

It was less than two minutes until Mathew Sterling appeared, 'Jack, good to see you,'

They shook hands and the MI6 chief, turned, 'Hello again, Tom.'

Tom smiled and shook hands, 'Mathew.'

'And this of course is Bogdan.'

'Hello, sir,' said the smiling Russian.

'Please. Call me, Mathew. Okay let's get you all through security and upstairs.'

In Sterling's office a large wall mounted television was showing graphic scenes from a breaking news story, 'What's this?' said Jack.

'This is why I couldn't meet you at Northolt. We've a pretty big flap on here,' said Mathew, then turning back to the television, continued, 'this happened about an hour ago.'

'That's Times Square,' said Tom.

'Correct. There's been a co-ordinated attack in New York and Tel Aviv. Both explosions happened at the same time.'

'Shahadi's bombs?' said Bogdan.

* * *

The news of the simultaneous disasters flashed around the world. The explosion in Times Square had caused a great deal of damage to the immediate area. Property and vehicles had been destroyed, and the initial body count was well over a hundred with twice as many left injured.

In the Ramat Aviv Mall the number of dead was greater than New York. The dome above the central food court had collapsed following the blast, and it was this which had caused more deaths than the blast itself.

Although both bombs had exploded and caused considerable carnage, neither one had gone nuclear.

Chapter Fifty Four
'The Hand-Over'

It had rained during the night, but the following morning was mild with a clear blue sky. In Jack and Nicole's Berkshire home, breakfast had been laid out on the patio, overlooking the lush landscaped gardens. The night before had been a mixture of celebration and regret. Shahadi was secure and his bombs, although devastating for America and Israel, failed to deliver the unthinkable.

Bogdan and Tom were at the breakfast table with Nicole, when Jack emerged from the house. 'That was Mathew on the phone. The Yanks and the Israelis have done initial forensics on the blast locations. Apparently they've found plutonium at the seat of the explosions.'

Tom put his cup down, 'So how come it was a conventional blast and not nuclear?'

'I asked the same question. Initial thoughts are, whoever built the bombs, designed them to explode, but without detonating the nuclear core.'

'A bomb maker with a conscience?' said Nicole.

Jack put his hand on his wife's shoulder, 'Or maybe someone who didn't trust Shahadi?'

The big Russian smiled, 'Anyway, is over now.'

Jack sat down, 'Not quite. Our friend Mr. Shahadi is being handed over to the Yanks later today. He's been transferred to Vauxhall Cross this morning.'

'Why aren't MI6 holding onto him?' said Tom.

'The Americans demanded they take him. I guess our lot are gonna let the Yanks do the donkey work getting the information from him. But Mathew said we're holding onto all the treasure.'

'What treasure, boss? Not my five million.'

Tom patted Bogdan on the back, 'Don't panic, big man, your five mill is safe. Treasure is spook talk for information, intelligence. The laptop, cell-phones and documents we took from Ras Wasin.'

Jack laughed and poured some tea, 'What time are your flights?'

'I'm on the fourteen hundred, to Dubai.'

'Da, Moscow flight is three fifteen.'

Nicole wiped her mouth with a soft linen napkin, 'Are you driving the guys to the airport, darling?'

'No. There's a chauffeur car coming. I'm going into London. I want to see Shahadi before he's whisked off to Langley.'

A little after ten thirty, the sleek Mercedes slipped out of the big gates and down the lane to the main road. Jack and Nicole had waved them off and were back in the house, 'Okay, baby. I'm gonna get changed, I'll be back this evening.'

'Don't be late, Jack. I've a lovely dinner planned and then an early night.'

He smiled and held her in his arms, then kissed her gently, 'I love you, Nicole.'

* * *

The windows in Mathew's office were open and Connor Reagan, the CIA's Head of Station in London, looked out over the River Thames, 'Great view, you guys have here.'

'Yes, quite,' said the MI6 chief.

'Okay, I guess we better get this guy outta here and over to our Embassy.'

Jack stood up, 'You're welcome to him. I hope they throw the book at him. I hope he rots in a cell for the rest of his life.'

The CIA man turned from the window, a bemused look on his tanned face, 'I doubt that. He's got too much valuable information on the terrorist organizations around the world; he's gonna do a deal.'

'You're fucking joking,' said Jack in disgust, 'after what he's done, he gets to walk away?'

'Pretty much, yeah. Once he's been debriefed, he'll be back on his yacht. Okay, thanks for everything, Mathew. Good working with you, sir.'

They shook hands, 'I'm sure we'll see each other again, Connor.'

The big American offered his hand to Jack, 'I'm coming down with you,' said Jack.

'Jack. What are you doing?'

'Don't worry, Matt. I just want a little word with our friend Mr. Shahadi before he leaves.'

At the main entrance to the Vauxhall Cross building, four shiny black people-carriers were lined up. Alongside each vehicle stood two very fit looking young men, all wore business suits and sun glasses, even though the sun had vanished into a cloudy sky several hours earlier.

In the foyer, Jack and Conner waited with three other CIA operatives for the arms dealer to arrive. Several silent minutes past and then a smiling Shahadi appeared, escorted by half a dozen MI6 security men.

Reagan stepped forward, 'Thank you, gentlemen. We'll take it from here.'

The Americans took hold of the smiling man and moved to the exit. Jack followed, and as the group left the building, the rain began to fall. At the bottom of the steps Shahadi looked over his shoulder, the thin smile ever present, 'I told you, Jack. Whatever I need to do to survive.'

Before the arms dealer entered the vehicle, Jack quickly moved forward. Grabbing his shoulder, he spun the man round. 'I'll be seeing you again . . .Vini. You're not getting away with Farida's murder. I don't give a shit what deal you do with these guys. I'm coming after you.'

Shahadi looked Jack straight in the eyes, then, as he opened his mouth to speak, Jack's face was suddenly splattered with blood. He instinctively turned away from the source of the spray, and, as he wiped the warm cloying mess from his eyes, his anger abated. Lying dead at his feet was the body of Vini Shahadi, the side of his head blown off, his lifeblood washing away with the afternoon rain.

On the roof of the apartment building, Danny Shomron said quietly, 'That's for you my darling, Farida.' He swiftly disassembled the high powered sniper rifle and quickly slotted each component into the fitted case. Before closing the lid, he took out the scope again and raised it to his eye. He carefully looked over the parapet at the scene three hundred yards away. Several men were running around, some taking cover behind vehicles, others with weapons drawn, all shouting into their wrist mics. But one man stood alone, looking down at the lifeless figure of Vini Shahadi. Danny refocused the scope onto the man's face and grinned. The man standing over the body was smiling . . .

The End

Epilogue

It was over a week since Vini Shahadi was shot on the steps of Vauxhall Cross. In Tel Aviv, Danny Shomron smiled as he read the article in *Artuz Sheva,* Israel's national newspaper. The report reflected badly on the British Secret Service and the CIA, in allowing a major player in the world of terrorism to be killed right on their doorstep. Shomron put down the broadsheet and stood up from the lounger. He strolled down the quiet beach and before stepping into the sea, stopped and looked up to the clear blue sky, 'Tonight at prayers, I shall say *Kaddish* for you, my darling Farida,' then slowly walked into the warm waters of the Mediterranean.

Akim al Hashem's widow and family, where relocated to Jordan. They were given a monthly income and a house in one of the nicer neighbourhoods in Amman.

Lisa Reynard spent ten days in the American Embassy's medical facility, after which she returned to her home in Washington. On the third day of sick-leave, Jack Castle rang her door bell. The huge arrangement of flowers he carried was almost too big to get through the front door.

The crews of Golden Cloud 2 and 3 were eventually released, as it was clear they had nothing to do with Shahadi's plot. The ships however were confiscated by the Americans and the Israelis respectively.

Marcel Dubois was unhappy to suddenly find himself unemployed, but only until an unexpected payment of two hundred thousand dollars appeared in his bank account.

Yossi, the manager of the charter company, was dismissed for losing a one hundred and twenty thousand dollar, Cessna aircraft. His employer was not all that worried, as he recovered a hundred and fifty thousand from the insurance.

Ahmed Benour had his maintenance crew strip all the weapons from the Hind gunship and re-paint the helicopter in the ALSOCO livery. The company paid him five hundred thousand dollars for the aircraft.

Bogdan's five million was deposited in the London branch of the *Banque Swisse de Geneve*.
On his return to Moscow his Ford Ranger truck had been towed away. He never bothered to get it out of the pound.

In Dubai, Tom's wife, Helen once again gave him grief over the wound on his upper arm,
'Every time you take off with Jack, it's always you that gets the scars.' Tom just smiled, kissed her, then took his yacht out into the Gulf.

After spending a couple of days with Lisa, Jack returned to London. He was excited when he and Nikki attended the maternity clinic, for her first scan. His excitement quickly turned to mild panic, when the nurse said Nikki was having twins.